"You're backing out already?" "Like you backed out of our relationship, Kim couldn't help but think.

"No, but after this evening it's clear your father doesn't want me here." Zane turned his head.

"I'm sorry for his behavior tonight. He hasn't taken this well at all."

"Years ago I forgave him, but he hasn't forgiven me for being poor nor the fact my father was often locked up for being drunk." He snapped his fingers. "Oh, wait. He probably wouldn't have cared about that if I hadn't dared to date his daughter."

She would have married Zane in spite of what her father felt, but Zane had never given her a chance. He'd left Hope and her. One night he was supposed to come pick her up for her senior prom, but he didn't show up. It wasn't until the next day she'd discovered Zane was gone. Then later she saw the check that her father had written to Zane.

"Was I only worth twenty thousand dollars to you?"

Books by Margaret Daley

Love Inspired

*Gold in the Fire
*A Mother for Cindy
*Light in the Storm
The Cinderella Plan
*When Dreams Come True
Hearts on the Line
*Tidings of Joy
Heart of the Amazon
†Once Upon a Family
†Heart of the Family
†Family Ever After
A Texas Thanksgiving
†Second Chance Family
†Together for the Holidays
††Love Lessons
††Heart of a Cowboy
††A Daughter for Christmas
**His Holiday Family
**A Love Rekindled

Love Inspired Suspense

So Dark the Night
Vanished
Buried Secrets
Don't Look Back
Forsaken Canyon
What Sarah Saw
Poisoned Secrets
Cowboy Protector
Christmas Peril
  "Merry Mayhem"
§Christmas Bodyguard
Trail of Lies
§Protecting Her Own
§Hidden in the Everglades

*The Ladies of Sweetwater Lake
†Fostered by Love
††Helping Hands Homeschooling
**A Town Called Hope
§Guardians, Inc.

MARGARET DALEY

feels she has been blessed. She has been married more than thirty years to her husband, Mike, whom she met in college. He is a terrific support and her best friend. They have one son, Shaun. Margaret has been writing for many years and loves to tell a story. When she was a little girl, she would play with her dolls and make up stories about their lives. Now she writes these stories down. She especially enjoys weaving stories about families and how faith in God can sustain a person when things get tough. When she isn't writing, she is fortunate to be a teacher for students with special needs. Margaret has taught for more than twenty years and loves working with her students. She has also been a Special Olympics coach and has participated in many sports with her students.

A Love Rekindled
Margaret Daley

Love Inspired

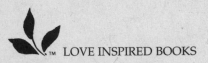

LOVE INSPIRED BOOKS

Recycling programs
for this product may
not exist in your area.

ISBN-13: 978-0-373-08230-8

A LOVE REKINDLED

www.LoveInspiredBooks.com

Printed in U.S.A.

Be of good courage, and He shall
strengthen your heart all ye that hope in the Lord.
—*Psalms* 31:24

To the people along the Gulf Coast

Chapter One

Clasping the strap of her purse so tightly pain zipped up her arm, Kim Walters zeroed in on Zane Davidson, the man she had avoided for the past three years since he had returned to Hope, the man who had broken her heart. The man she wished she never had to talk to again. But he was her last hope to get her house repaired at a price she could afford.

Before she lost her nerve, she crossed the parking lot of the hurricane-damaged school building where she was a third-grade teacher. *I can do this.* But her step faltered the closer she came to Zane. The fingernails on her hand around her purse strap dug into her palm.

This is crazy. Maggie is wrong. My cousin is an eternal optimist. Surely there's another solution to getting our home restored. Kim halted, chewing on her bottom lip.

I can't do this.

Before he saw her, she started to turn to leave. But she was too late. His dark blue gaze—that used to draw her in and hold her captive—snagged hers from across the parking lot. He said something to one of the workers next to him, then strode toward her.

She froze, wanting to leave, knowing she couldn't now. She wouldn't show any emotions to him. She didn't want him to realize his leaving Hope fifteen years ago had crushed her. Shifting, about to face him head-on, she squared her shoulders and lifted her chin, hoping to give the illusion she was taller than her five feet four inches.

"It's nice to see you, Kim." He stopped a

yard away from her, a neutral expression on his face.

"It is?" she asked before she could censor her words. Open hostility was no way to get him to agree to what she wanted—especially since she'd visited all the contractors in Hope she trusted and they couldn't do her repairs for months.

"I've been back three years, and this is the first time you and I have talked."

"We move in different circles." As a teenager, she remembered her father kept telling her that she and Zane were from different social classes and a relationship would never work between them. They were too mismatched.

The hard line of his jaw attested to the effect the reminder of the gulf between them had on Zane. He drew in a deep breath that released the rigid set to his shoulders. "How's your dad?"

Surprised for a few seconds at his question, she averted her gaze, trying to formulate an answer. Zane and her father had never gotten along. Fifteen years ago, she'd been ready to defy her father for Zane. But then he'd left her without an explanation, taking the decision out of her hands. "Since you've been in Hope for a while, I'm sure you've heard about his illness."

"Yes. I knew a guy with Parkinson's disease in New Orleans. It's tough. How's he coping?"

"He's hanging in there." She didn't want to talk about her father and needed to steer the conversation quickly to what she wanted to discuss—her family home, Bienville, restored. Memories of Hurricane Naomi hitting Hope almost three months ago flashed into her mind, battering at her composure like the storm had her home. "I need you to give me an estimate on repairing Bienville. The hurricane flooded the first floor of the house and did extensive wind damage to the roof. We have done what we can, but there's still a lot that needs to be done by a professional."

"I thought you had someone working on your home."

"Henderson Roofing and Construction left town."

"When are they coming back?"

"Never." She gritted her teeth to keep from explaining further. It was bad enough her father and family had been taken by a crook, but she didn't want to admit it to this man.

Zane's eyes narrowed. "I hadn't heard that. Is there a problem?"

"It just happened yesterday. The problem is our gaping roof."

"Most of the town needs repair."

The wind off the water not far from Jefferson Elementary School chilled Kim, reminding her of the cold, damp rooms in her family home. "I realize that, but Henderson Roofing removed part of the old roof to replace it, making the problem worse since they skipped town. I need that repaired immediately before it rains again. My father isn't doing well and—" she swallowed hard, fighting the tears swelling into her throat "—I know you probably have more work than you need, but…but we're only living in a few rooms right now."

"My crews are stretched as thin as possible. I just don't see—"

"I understand. Thank you." Whirling around, she marched toward her eight-year-old sedan. She couldn't stay another second or she would cry in front of Zane Davidson, and she'd promised herself she would never let him be the reason she shed a tear again.

Somehow she made it to her car and slipped inside. Tears flooded her eyes as she started the engine. When she spied him coming toward her, she gunned the Lexus and sped away from the school. Heat flamed her cheeks at the same time wet tracks streaked down her face.

Zane stared at Kim's car as it sped away. He'd seen the sheen of tears in her eyes and wanted to dismiss their effect on him.

He hadn't been prepared to talk to Kim again. He wasn't sure he ever would be, and since returning to Hope, he had purposefully stayed away from any event she might be attending. When he'd been approached about repairing the hurricane-damaged school he'd attended as a child, he'd almost turned it down because Kim was a teacher there now. Hope, Mississippi, was a small town of twenty thousand, and he shouldn't have come back home, but he had something to prove to the town.

Fifteen years ago he hadn't been good enough for Kim Walters. Now the same people who had taken pleasure in pointing that out to him were the very ones who wanted to do business with him. But he'd never wanted to prove his worth at the expense of a hurricane destroying much of the town. Even though Hope had managed to get back on its feet, parts of it still looked as if the storm had struck only yesterday. In the three years since he'd returned, he had come to care for the people as he hadn't when he'd lived here as an angry teenager. However, seeing and dealing with Kim on a daily basis was a whole different story.

Shaking the memories from his thoughts, he strolled toward his mobile office at the school site. He didn't allow himself to think about the past often. All it would do was stir his anger, and since he'd found the Lord, he knew there was a better way. But now he wondered if God was testing him when He put Kim in his path.

"Boss, the rest of the floodlights have arrived. This should help us make our three-week deadline," his secretary said.

"Thanks, Susan. I don't know what I would have done if it weren't for you. Everyone wants everything done yesterday."

"Yeah. There aren't enough hours in the day to do what you need to do, but then work is about all there is to do here."

He sat in his desk chair and looked across the trailer at his right-hand woman. "It's been three years. I thought you would be settled in by now. Do you regret following me to Hope?"

Susan Fayard twisted her mouth into a

thoughtful expression and tapped the side of her chin. "Well, there are days like this one I long for the quieter pace of New Orleans."

"New Orleans quieter? That's the first time I've heard that."

"I thought you were only going to build the hotel and pier in Gulfport. That was three years and several major projects ago. Are you ever going back to New Orleans?"

"Maybe, but Hope is halfway between our New Orleans and Mobile offices. Good location to manage both. Do you want me to transfer you back to New Orleans?"

"No, boss. I'm fine for the time being. It's just for the past three months we have been working nonstop."

"There's a lot to rebuild and not enough hours to do it all." The picture of Kim as she'd stood before him earlier materialized in his mind, her chin tilted up, her posture so straight and proper he'd wondered when she would snap. But then he'd looked into her soft blue eyes and glimpsed the sorrow of the past few months—the toll the hurricane had taken on her and so many others in town. "Maybe after the school is finished you can take a little time off."

"I've gone back to New Orleans for a couple of weekends since the hurricane. That's enough for now. I'll let you know when I've had enough and yearn for more than Hope has to offer."

Zane chuckled. "Look out, New Orleans, when that happens."

The opening door halted his secretary's reply. When she saw the visitor was Gideon O'Brien, a good friend of his, her smile of welcome grew. "You've come to rescue me from my tyrant boss."

"It's almost five. I thought I would stop by here on the way to Broussard Park and pick you up," Gideon said to Zane. "If I didn't, you'd probably forget."

"You know me well. I had forgotten. I was just about to return some calls, but they can wait. Nothing beats a good game of basketball to relieve stress."

Gideon's eyebrow rose. "Stress? From all I've seen, you're Mr. Cool. Nothing much rattles you."

Talking to Kim Walters earlier had stressed him. Her appearance had taken him by surprise. He hadn't been prepared to see her. She had been the one reason he had hesitated coming back to Hope when he'd gotten the opportunity to work on some construction projects along the Gulf Coast where he'd grown up.

"How about more work than I can handle?"

"That's a good thing. That shouldn't stress you. You say no to who you have to. If you can't do it, you can't."

Zane pushed to his feet. He could remember Kim's look when he had turned down her offer to restore her home. It had gripped his heart and squeezed it. "Yeah, that's all I can do. There are only twenty-four hours in a day." But what did he do with the guilt from saying no?

"And for the next hour you're gonna forget about work."

"Where are Jared and Kip?" Being with Gideon and his friend's soon-to-be step-sons gave him a sense of what it would be like to have a family. That was all he needed to fulfill any yearning he might have to be a father. It was right for Gideon but not him.

"Out in the car, so we'd better book it."

"I'll be back at six," Zane said to Susan as he headed for the door right behind Gideon.

"I'll be gone by then, boss. Helping to plan the reopening of this elementary school. It's gonna be a big celebration."

He paused in the doorway. "A celebration?" That was the first he'd heard of it.

"Friday night before Fat Tuesday. Think Mardi Gras, treasure hunts, food. All kinds of fun. So I guess this place better be ready by then."

"No pressure there," Zane mumbled to himself as he closed the trailer door. If the weather cooperated and the supplies he needed arrived on schedule, he would barely make that deadline.

Jared and Kip sat in his friend's Jeep, a frown on their faces. Zane liked children as long as they belonged to someone else. He didn't see himself ever being a father. His hadn't been the best example. If he had lived a hundred years ago, his dad would have been referred to as the town drunk.

When he climbed into the front passenger seat, he shifted around and greeted Gideon's fiancée's sons. "Which one of you drew the short straw?"

Kip raised his hand. "Me."

"Oh, sorry, you've gotta partner with me."

Kip shot his brother a narrow-eyed look. "That's okay. I don't care if we lose except Jared cheated. He peeked when he shouldn't have."

"Did not."

"Yes, you did."

Gideon started his Jeep. "We can always go back to your grandmother's."

Jared snapped his mouth closed and turned his head to stare out the window. Kip glared at him for a few more seconds then did likewise.

"Ah, silence," Zane said with a chuckle.

"Savor it. It won't last." Gideon pulled out of his parking space near the trailer. "That's why we're playing basketball. Kathleen, her mother and Miss Alice are planning the wedding and were having a hard time."

"Jared started it," Kip piped in.

"Did not."

Zane listened to the two boys banter back and forth before Gideon said, "That's it. No more warnings. We'll go straight home after the park. No stopping for hamburgers."

Again Jared and Kip clammed up, and the second Gideon came to a halt in the parking lot, they jumped out of the backseat and raced for the basketball court. Kip took a shot. When he rebounded the ball, Jared tried to wrestle it away from him.

"Shouldn't you go referee or something?" Zane asked, watching the boys playing tug-of-war with the ball.

"Nope. Let them tire themselves out. Sometimes they just have to use up the extra energy they have, especially after school. It takes all their best behavior to sit still during class. Kip does pretty well. Jared is a work in progress."

"How do you do it? They aren't your children."

Gideon peered at Zane. "They will be. I'm adopting them right after Kathleen and I get married."

"Not only are you abandoning bachelorhood but you're going to be a parent. What's come over you?" Zane asked with a laugh.

"Love. I love Kathleen. And I love those two boys. You wait. It could happen to you."

The vision of Kim teased his thoughts. He pushed it away. "No. Not me. I like being a bachelor. Just look at my busy schedule. When would I have time to fall in love?"

"When it's important, you'll make time."

Marriage wasn't high on his list, so he didn't have to worry about that. He still could remember the last time he'd returned to Hope—close to a year after he'd left at the age of nineteen. He'd come to challenge Kim's father and ask her to elope with him only to discover Kim was engaged to a proper Southern gentleman—the kind her father approved of. He left that same day, without even seeing her, and hadn't come back until three years ago when he found out that she wasn't married to that proper Southern gentleman anymore. His reaction to that news—mostly anger that she'd thrown away their relationship for the "right" guy and the marriage hadn't even worked—made him even more wary.

And in the time he'd been in Hope, he had avoided Kim and her family, not wanting to deal with what happened in the past or the feelings he'd once had for her—strong ones. He had thought she would be the woman he would spend the rest of his life with in spite of the fact a lot of people thought they didn't belong together. Maybe they hadn't, but that hadn't changed how he felt about Kim.

He shouldn't let what they once had dictate what he did now. She needed help. He tried not to turn people away if he could figure out a way to help them. Allan Prescott had been there for him when he'd left Hope an angry young man. He had hired him to work in his New Orleans construction company and taught him everything he knew. Then when Allan had retired, he'd given him an opportunity to take over the business.

He had made something of himself since leaving Hope because of Allan and the help the man had given him. Now Kim and her father—the man who hadn't thought he was good enough to marry her—needed his help. The tables were turned. His business was doing great while Kim's family had lost theirs. *Can I forget the past and be around Kim on a daily basis to make the repairs she needs?*

"Mom, you're home *finally*. Papa Keith isn't feeling well. He's taking a nap." Kim's ten-year-old daughter Anna sat at the kitchen table drinking milk and eating cookies.

"When did he lie down?" Exhausted after her encounter with Zane earlier, Kim set her purse on the counter then sank onto a chair across from her child.

"When I came home from school." Anna popped in the last bite and gulped down the rest of the milk, then hopped up. "Gotta run. I'm helping Maggie with the garden."

"It's January."

"Yeah, but she said she'll be planting some vegetables by the end of February. The garden is a mess since the hurricane."

She shouldn't be surprised that her cousin would be out working in the garden the first chance she got. After the hurricane, Maggie had focused on the yard while Kim had turned her full attention to the house. Bienville was the family estate—what little was left of it—but they each took care of different parts of it. "Did you get your homework done?"

"Not yet, but I won't be outside too long. It'll be dark soon. Besides, it's Friday. I have all weekend."

As her daughter darted out the door that led to the outside staircase to the ground level, Kim placed her folded arms on the table and rested her head on them. What was she going to do? Could she do the repairs herself with Maggie's help?

She rolled to her feet and headed into the rest of the upstairs part of the antebellum house that had been in her family for generations. When she opened the door to what had once been her bedroom, she peered up at the gaping hole in the ceiling covered with a tarp to protect the interior until she could have the roof put on. That had been the one thing the contractor her father had hired was supposed to repair right away. The roof had been riddled with holes from missing shingles and several trees and limbs that had landed on it. A tarp wasn't as effective as a good roof.

The house was unlivable except for two bedrooms, a bathroom and a game room/ now kitchen upstairs, all beneath the third-story attic that had added another layer of protection from the elements. The other second-story rooms, like her bedroom, had been exposed because of the damage produced by Hurricane Naomi. Add that to the fact the downstairs had been flooded during the storm. In all the hurricanes that Bienville had gone through, this was the first time water had come into the house. The three inches had been enough to cause major problems since they didn't have flood insurance.

Right after the storm, she'd managed to repair and clean up the middle section of the upstairs so they could live in those rooms. But the downstairs had been filled with muck and debris. In the time since Hurricane Naomi, she, along with her family, had finally sanitized and aired the flooded part while still teaching her third-grade class in a temporary shelter and taking care of her father whose health had declined. There had been a time when her family had had a lot of money and would have been able to pay for the work to be done immediately. But not now.

Before going back to the makeshift kitchen to start dinner, Kim eased the door open to the bedroom her father shared with his grandnephew, Brady, Maggie's twelve-year-old son. Her dad was sleeping more and more, and lately he hardly left his room except for meals. Every time he saw the condition of his home, something died inside him—piece by piece. Worry over her father's state of mind and health plagued her.

All she could think of doing was somehow getting his house back to its original condition, which took money they didn't have. Insurance had paid for the roof to be repaired, but the contractor had skipped town with the money her dad had given him to buy the supplies.

She peeked into the bedroom and caught sight of her father sitting on the side of the bed, his shoulders hunched. He stared at the floor at his feet, looking every bit of his sixty years. More wrinkles had appeared on his face, and his black hair had additional gray. Since the storm, a pasty pallor to his features, mainly because he never went outside anymore, underscored her father's struggle to keep going each day.

"Dad, can I get you anything?"

He lifted his head, and bleakness stared back at her until he glanced toward the large floor-to-ceiling window. "Is dinner ready?"

"Not yet. I was late coming home. I'm going to make it right now."

"It's awfully quiet in here. Where is everyone?"

"Anna is outside helping Maggie. I don't know where Brady is, but he ought to be home soon since it's near dinnertime."

Her dad stared at the cot Maggie's son slept on near the only window that let in outside light. "He came flying in here right before I took a nap. I think he's over at a friend's house, so don't count on him for dinner."

"Why don't you come and keep me company while I cook?"

"I'll pass. I might watch the news or something." He clutched the post on the bed and pulled himself up, then covered the distance to the TV and switched it on, his hand shaking.

"Okay, Dad. I'll come get you when it's time."

"Maybe I'll eat in here tonight." Defeat echoed in his words.

Kim came into the room and went to her father. "I'll get the house repaired. I reported the contractor to the police today. They may be able to recover our money, if they can find him. In the meantime, we'll do the work ourselves."

Her father looked at her as if she were

crazy. "We will? Do you know what to do? I certainly don't."

"I bought the book *Do-It-Yourself Guide to Home Repairs* this afternoon." This was after Zane turned her down. "We're intelligent. We'll be able to figure it out." Although after thumbing through it, she had her doubts.

"Speak for yourself. The few times I've used a hammer I caused more problems than I fixed."

"I don't think we're going to have a choice. Bob has said he'll help when he can, but he's working on his own home."

"Bob's a good neighbor, but he's no better off than we are." Her dad rocked back and forth, his hands still trembling. "There's just so much to be done."

"I know, Dad. We'll get it done." *I hope.* Kim walked toward the hallway. "I'd better get dinner started, and I expect you to come eat with us. It isn't good to stay in this room all the time."

He grumbled something under his breath. "I'll have everything ready in an hour."

Kim threw her dad a smile over her shoulder then pulled the door closed. If he wasn't in the temporary kitchen when it was time to eat, she would be back in here to coax him out of the room. She didn't want him to become a recluse, but she wasn't sure she could prevent it.

Back in the game room/kitchen she opened the refrigerator and studied its contents. Reaching for the thawed ground beef, Kim decided on spaghetti, one of the few dishes she'd mastered. Anna loved it. After removing the ingredients, she plopped the ground beef in the skillet and began browning it.

While that was cooking, she started dicing a big yellow onion. The potent aroma watered her eyes. Tears leaked from them and ran down her cheeks. She continued slicing while occasionally swiping the back of her hand across her cheeks. She and onions didn't get along. This always happened, but tonight the release of tears was a relief.

A knock at the outside door to the game

room sounded. She hurried to finish the last part of the onion before answering. Another rap echoed through the quiet. Finished finally, she dumped the diced pieces into the skillet and hurried toward the door, dabbing a dish towel on her face to erase any evidence of her tears. But her hands smelled strongly of onion, which only prompted more wet rivulets to run down her cheeks.

She paused to rub the towel one last time over her face when the door flew open and Anna came in.

"Mom, there's a man here to see you."

She forced a shaky smile to her face and tossed the towel onto the counter. "Thanks, honey."

Anna whirled around and raced back outside, leaving her alone with Zane.

Chapter Two

For a few seconds, Kim's red eyes and
tear-streaked cheeks rooted Zane in the
doorway. He shouldn't have come. He
should have ignored the little voice in his
head that kept telling him he needed to
help her so that once and for all he could
put his past behind him.

Feeling the drill of her stunned gaze finally caused him to ask, "Can I come in?"

She blinked, then turned away. "Why
are you here?"

Her tightly controlled voice, one he remembered her using when she was upset,
coupled with the tears compelled him

to finish what he'd started by coming to her home. "I've changed my mind. I think I can help you." Somehow he would manage it—not for her but for him.

She took a couple of steps back then swept around and hurried to the stove. "Come in." Using a wooden spoon, she stirred the ground beef browning in the skillet then added some spices and diced tomatoes.

The aroma of meat, onions and garlic wafted to him and made his stomach rumble. He'd forgotten to eat lunch again. His mouth watered, and he swallowed hard. He moved toward what Kim was using as a kitchen with a small sink, a refrigerator and stove at one end. In the year he'd known and dated Kim, he'd never been in this room, which looked like a game room, and only a couple of times had he been in her home. The last visit—or rather summons—was seared into his memories. For years it fueled his determination to prove himself to the people of Hope, especially Kim's father.

Now, though, he realized how unimportant that had been. But it had taken the Lord's guidance to show him that.

She turned on the oven and removed some French bread from its wrapper, then rotated toward him. "What changed your mind?"

"I figured I owe you."

She leaned back against the bar counter, gripping it. "How so?"

"For the time we knew each other. We were…friends once and friends help each other."

"I thought you were all booked up."

"I am."

"Then how?"

"I'll do the work myself—at least until I can hire more workers."

She swung toward the sink, her back to him, as she filled a pot with water. "I can't let you do that," she said, again with that tightly controlled voice.

"Do you want my help or not?"

After putting the pot on a burner and switching the stove on, she faced him.

"How can you be here and on your other construction sites? I know you're doing the school and several other places in Hope."

"Five other ones and several in Gulfport and Biloxi, but that's my problem. Not yours. I can work here in the afternoon and early evening. That's all I can do. If you want to find someone else, I understand."

She laughed, but there was no humor in the sound. "That worked well the last time we hired someone. Henderson and his crew skipped town with the down payment."

"I won't be skipping town."

That sharp blue gaze zoomed in on him. "You did once."

She was having second thoughts now that he had decided to help her? He gritted his teeth, wishing he'd kept his mouth shut. "That's in the past. I'm not that person anymore. Do you want my help or not?"

"How much will you charge?"

"I'll have you pay for the supplies." He knew about the financial problems that her family had gone through in the past ten years, which was part of the reason he'd decided to come see her. Like many in Hope, she was strapped for money, especially in the aftermath of the hurricane.

"And?"

"When we're through, I'll let you come up with what's fair."

The color leached from her face. "What if I decide to give you nothing else?"

"I've always known you to be fair, and from what I've heard about you in the past few years, that hasn't changed."

"When can you start? As you probably saw when you arrived, there's only a tarp covering the gaping hole where the roof was over my bedroom and that section of the house. If it rains like they predict in a few days, we may have as much water in here as we did during the hurricane."

"I can start tomorrow afternoon. Did they leave any supplies? I didn't see any in the yard."

"No, even though we paid them for the shingles. They'd done some work for others around here so I didn't think they would leave Hope like that." Kim placed the bread on a baking sheet and stuck it in the oven.

"I've asked around and discovered a couple of the people they worked for are having problems now."

Red patches colored her cheeks, rivaling her red hair. "When did you hear this?"

"I made some calls before I came."

"Why?"

"I don't like companies like that one coming into the area and taking advantage of what happened here. Most are reputable, but this one wasn't. They used inferior supplies and cut corners. Two of their customers had gone to the police about it. I think that's why they skipped town."

"Oh." Her shoulders sagged. "Why didn't I hear about this?"

"Because our police chief only heard from the second dissatisfied customer this morning. The other one two days ago. The chief had gone out to talk to the owner of the company, but one of Henderson's workers said his boss was in Biloxi buying supplies. The chief had planned to talk with him today."

"And in the meantime Mr. Henderson left town permanently."

"That's pretty much what our police chief thinks, too."

"When I talked with him today, he didn't tell me there had been two other complaints." She glanced toward the pot, the water in it boiling. She pulled open the cabinet behind her and withdrew a box of spaghetti, then put the pasta into the pot. "How come he told you?"

"I asked Ian if he'd heard anything from anyone else in town. Did you?"

Her face reddened even more. "I'm not very good at this business stuff. Dad used to handle it, but his Parkinson's is getting worse."

"So I've heard."

She straightened. "What else have you heard?"

"The usual gossip that floats around this town."

"Since when have you listened to gossip?"

"I don't pay much attention, especially since I know what it means to be the object of that gossip." He'd been bothered by the fact people were discussing Keith Sommerfield, even if the man had made his life difficult years ago.

She pressed her lips together in a tight line. "I need you to realize Dad will be here while you're working. He rarely leaves the house anymore. Do you still want to personally do the work?"

"Will your father be able to handle me being here? Does he know you asked me?"

Glancing toward the stove, Kim covered the few feet and stirred the meat sauce. "No. I thought I would tell him if you agreed."

"Yeah, why get him upset if I refuse?"

"Right," she answered although he really hadn't asked a question.

"Then I suggest you talk to him before I show up for work tomorrow."

"It's Saturday. I'll be here."

"To smooth the rough waters?"

She sighed. "He'll understand we have limited options. At the very least, the roof has to be put on."

"What's going on here?" came a raspy voice from the doorway into the hall.

Kim sank back against the counter, the sight of her father in the entrance jamming her throat. All words fled her mind while she watched her dad move into the game room, his gaze glued to Zane's face.

"I repeat, what's going on here?"

"I was just leaving," Zane said, stepping back toward the outside door.

"Please, stay." Kim pivoted toward her father. "Dad, Zane has agreed to fix our roof. Isn't that great?" She poured as much enthusiasm as she could into her voice, but that didn't stop her father's scowl from deepening. This would have to work because they didn't have any other choices at the moment except repairing the place themselves.

"Since when?"

"Since Mr. Henderson left town." She wanted to say to her father that she'd given him a chance to get the house fixed and now it was her turn. But she bit her bottom lip to keep those words inside. She didn't need to remind him Mr. Henderson had been his choice. Before her dad said anything else, she returned her attention to Zane. "I've forgotten my manners. Please, stay for dinner. We can talk about tomorrow afterward. The least I can do is feed you since you're squeezing us into your busy schedule."

Zane's gaze captured hers, boring into her. "I don't want to intrude on your family time."

"Nonsense. You should meet everyone since you'll be around here. We're having spaghetti, and if I remember correctly, that's one of your favorite dishes."

"Kim, if the man doesn't want to stay, then—"

"I'll stay. Spaghetti is still one of my favorite meals. When did you learn to cook?"

Zane's attention never left her face as though they were the only two in the room. But she was very aware of her father only a few feet from her. She didn't have to look at him to realize anger vibrated from him. She cleared her throat and said, "In the last five years."

"Weren't you the one who hated Foods and Nutrition in high school?"

"It was the teacher, not the subject." She switched off the burners, then walked to the back door and shouted for Anna and Maggie to come inside for dinner.

When she pivoted toward her dad and Zane, they were having a staring contest. She'd never known her father to back down, but after a half a minute, he spun on his heel and left the kitchen without a word.

Zane's gaze latched on to hers. "I'd better leave."

"No. I invited you to dinner, and you accepted. You're a guest in this house whether you like it or not."

One corner of his mouth lifted. "Don't make it sound like it's the worst thing that can happen to me."

It may not be for you, but it is for me. Why did I ask? What am I trying to prove to Dad by asking you to dinner? Before she could say anything, the back door opened and in poured three kids and Kim's cousin, Maggie Sommerfield.

"Anna wanted Polly to eat dinner with us. I said it was okay." Maggie shed her work gloves and put them on the desk off to the side.

"Sure. I made plenty. Zane is staying. He's agreed to repair the roof starting tomorrow." Kim tore her gaze from Zane and gave her cousin a weak smile. "I see Brady made it home in time for dinner, too."

"Yeah, barely. I'm starved," Anna said,

then Polly, her best friend who lived next door, chimed in with, "Me, too."

"Then go wash up and get Papa Keith for dinner." Kim dumped the spaghetti into a strainer in the sink.

"Hi, Maggie. It's good to see you again." Zane grinned at her cousin. "Is this your son?"

"Yes. Brady, this is Zane Davidson. We went to school together way back in the dark ages." She slid her attention from her son to Zane. "He was just telling me I don't know what I'm talking about when it comes to school, that things are different than when I was in middle school."

"Since we're the same age, I'm feeling old all of a sudden." Zane stuck his hand out and shook Brady's. "Nice to meet you. Your mom and I shared a couple of classes together."

"Nice to meet you, sir."

Zane laughed. "If I didn't feel old before, I do now."

As Zane and Brady began discussing the changes at the middle school,

Maggie went to the sink and washed her hands, leaning close to Kim to whisper, "Not only has he agreed to help with the house, you've managed to get him to stay for dinner. Fast work. I'm impressed." A sparkle danced in her eyes.

"Shh. He'll hear. And the only work I'm doing is getting this place finally taken care of."

When Kim grabbed her oven mitts and took the bread out, Anna and Polly came back into the room, tugging on Kim's dad's hand. "I told you two I wasn't hungry. I haven't changed my mind since you dragged me in here."

"Papa Keith, it's safe. Mom fixed spaghetti. She knows how to make that."

Heat scorched Kim's cheeks.

Her father's attention shifted from one person's face to another until it finally rested on Kim's. His gaze penetrated through her. "We have a lot to talk about later."

"Fine, we will. After we eat." Kim refused to back down from her dad. She would make him see there was no other option, and he was going to have to live with the arrangement. "Zane, since you're our guest, you can serve yourself first."

Zane started toward Kim, stopped and faced her father. "There's nothing we can do about what happened in the past. I have put it behind me."

Kim sensed a challenge being issued to her father, and he wasn't liking it one bit. He frowned and shuffled toward the table to get his plate, then hung back from the others.

Anna tugged on Kim's arm, and she bent down. "What happened in the past?" Anna whispered loud enough that everyone in the room heard.

"Honey, nothing important now." Kim pasted a smile on her face, the strain of it quivering the corners of her mouth.

"Ah, you never tell me anything."

She tweaked Anna's nose. "It isn't any of your business."

Five minutes later, everyone was served except her father who waited to be last. He approached the stove with his plate. His hand quaked. Kim watched, ready to step in and help. He was trembling more than usual, which only meant he was stressed and upset. She shouldn't have asked Zane to dinner, on top of everything else. But if he was going to be repairing their home, her father needed to be civil and get used to Zane being here.

The alternative was having a rain-soaked upstairs that leaked down into the ground floor, which had finally dried out. She had only recently gotten rid of the moldy, musty smell that permeated the whole place since the storm.

When her father took his chair at the head of the table, everyone began eating. Zane bowed his head and closed his eyes for a moment, then picked up his fork and speared some spaghetti.

Was Zane a Christian? One of the fights they'd had when they'd been dating was over her faith. She'd wanted to get married in the church. Zane hadn't wanted to have anything to do with a religious ceremony. Maggie had mentioned to her once that Zane was going to Hope Community Church now, which had only reinforced Kim's reason for staying away. For the past ten years, she'd seen less evidence of the Lord in people's lives. Life had become one series of struggles after another. The hurricane only confirmed that.

Anna looked at Zane and broke the silence that had descended at the table. "How do you know my mom?"

Kim's father snorted. When he brought his fork to his mouth, his hand quavered so badly he had to put it back on his plate without tasting the food. His gaze drilled into Kim, who curled her fingers around her napkin in her lap.

Zane finished eating his bite. "We dated once."

Anna's eyes grew round. "You did? What happened?"

"Anna!" Her daughter's curiosity would be the death of Kim—from embarrassment.

"But, Mom, you never tell me anything

about when you were growing up. Papa Keith has, but you haven't."

"He has?" Kim glanced at her dad, who hunched over his plate, his head down.

Anna gulped down some milk. "Yeah, going through some of those boxes in the attic got me to wondering about what you did when you were a kid."

"I've told you. I grew up in this home. Except for a few years when I was married to your father, I've lived here my whole life. It's been in our family for over a hundred and fifty years. That's why it's so important to get it repaired properly."

"Do you fix a lot of houses?" Anna asked Zane.

"Yes. I'm going to start on your roof tomorrow."

"I can help you." Brady tore off a piece of bread and chewed it.

"Me, too." Anna beamed. "I've never been on the roof."

A vision of her daughter standing three stories above the ground paraded across

Kim's mind. "And you aren't going to start now."

"Ah, Mom, why not? We can all pitch in and help fix this house up."

"That's what Mom and Dad are doing. They let me help when I'm not in school," Polly added while scooping up her last bite of spaghetti.

Everyone looked at Kim, including her dad and Zane. She fought the urge to squirm. Her daughter was right. If they all helped as much as possible, Zane would be gone faster and their home could be restored to the way it was.

Kim focused on her daughter, ignoring all the other stares. "I can't have you up on the roof."

Anna pouted. "That doesn't mean I can't do something."

"I'm sure I could find something for Anna to do if that's all right with you, Kim."

Oh, sure. Just come in and take over. When she had gone in desperation to ask him to help her today, she hadn't envisioned him being here day in and day out. She'd thought maybe he would supervise from a distance—a long distance.

"We have been working on the house and yard. You should have seen it right after the hurricane." With work, seeing to everyone in the house and her father's illness, Kim had little time to do all she had needed to do, but she'd tried.

"I did see it right after the hurricane."

The thought that Zane had come by and looked at her place threw her off-kilter. What else had he done? Did he know about the past fifteen years? About her failed marriage?

Her father scraped back his chair on the wooden floor and struggled to his feet. "I'm done."

With his hand on the table, he turned toward the door and started for it. At the sight of his unsteady gait, Kim rose at the same time Zane did. Her father reached for the bookcase by the exit but missed and went down. Zane rushed to him a few paces ahead of her.

"Let me help you." Zane put his arm around her father and raised him up partway.

Dad glared at Zane and yanked away. He would have gone down again if Zane hadn't secured his hold on her father.

She hurried to his side. "You need help."

"Not him." Tears glistened in her dad's eyes. "Please."

Kim glanced at Zane. "I can do it from here. Thanks for helping."

Zane backed off a few feet while Kim fought to get her father to a standing position, then locked her arms about him and assisted him out of the room. When she peered back, Zane stood there, his jaw clamped in an inflexible line. But in his eyes she saw pity. That look fired her anger.

When she left her father's bedroom after making sure he was resting, Kim made her way downstairs. Large sheets of plastic cordoned off the damaged part of the house from the livable area. She couldn't go back into the game room. By the time she did, she wanted Zane gone. She didn't want the man's pity about what was going on here. She needed his help but not any emotional investment for him—or her.

Stepping out on the veranda that ran the length of the front of the house, Kim drew in a deep breath of the cool winter air, laced with a salty aroma. Night blanketed the terrain, but in the distance, between the sounds of cars, she could hear the water lapping up on the beach. That sound always calmed her. She sank down on the top stair next to one of the stone lions that guarded her home. Their worn surface had weathered over the years, but they had stayed in place when the water came inside from the Gulf. Seeing them the next morning after the storm passed had given her hope that all the damage she'd seen inside could be fixed.

But three months later she wasn't so sure. They had scrubbed all the rooms downstairs, stripped away the rot and aired the place for weeks. Only recently had their neighbor's moisture meter indicated everything was dry. Now it was time to restore the interior. That required money they didn't have.

"We need to talk."

Zane's voice pierced her tranquility, robbing her of the peace the sound of the ocean had brought her. "I know but can we tomorrow? Today has been long and tiring."

"I want to get a few things settled tonight. If we can't work it out, I don't see how I can make the repairs." He folded his long length on the step beside her and rested his elbows on his jean-clad thighs, loosely clasping his hands.

From the light streaming through the open front door, she glimpsed his face. "You're backing out already?" *Like you backed out of our relationship?*

"No, but after this evening it's clear your father doesn't want me here. I didn't expect to be warmly welcomed into your home, but I can't work if he causes problems or gets too upset every time he sees me. It's evident he's having physical problems, and I won't be responsible for something happening to him if he gets stressed. It isn't a big secret your dad and I don't get along."

"I'm sorry for his behavior tonight. He hasn't taken this well at all. I've tried to get some counseling for him, but he'll have none of it. Right after the hurricane, I found him in the living room. He stood in a few inches of water, stunned and weeping. I've never seen him do that."

"Years ago I forgave him, but he hasn't forgiven me for being poor or the son of a drunkard." He snapped his fingers. "Oh, wait. He probably wouldn't have cared about that if I hadn't dared to date his daughter."

She would have married Zane in spite of what her father had felt, but Zane had never given her a chance. He'd left Hope and her. One night he was supposed to come pick her up for her senior prom, but he didn't show up. It wasn't until the next day she'd discovered Zane was gone. Then later she saw the check that her father had written to Zane.

"Was I only worth twenty thousand dollars to you?"

Chapter Three

Zane rose, her accusation blasting him in the face. "What do you mean? Twenty thousand dollars?"

"Not long after you left, when I went to get a check for Mom to pay the housekeeper, I saw the stub of the check my dad wrote you for twenty thousand dollars." Kim wouldn't let him have a height advantage on her. She stood and took the top stair so they were eye to eye. "It was written the day before you disappeared."

"I didn't disappear. My father knew where I was going."

"I asked him. He didn't tell me."

"Because I made him promise not to."

"Why?" The anger that had festered for years came to the surface, welling up from deep inside her.

"We weren't meant to be together. We were from two different worlds. I thought at one time we could ignore our differences and love would conquer all. I was wrong. I didn't even have any money to take you to prom in the style you were accustomed to. The tux I had managed to borrow for the dance didn't fit me. I stood in front of the mirror and saw someone I didn't like. Someone who was trying to be what he wasn't."

"Did my father ever offer you money?"

"Yes, but I'm not that type of person. He made it clear he would use all his power to break us up."

"Why didn't you tell me?"

"Because family meant so much to you. I didn't want to come between y'all. I thought with time he would see that with hard work I could make something of myself. But the reason I didn't show up for prom was because I was sitting in jail. The police officer said I ran a stop sign. My one phone call was to you. Your father answered, and he told me my problems had just begun, that he was going to make my life miserable, especially if I did anything wrong, even something as simple as running a stop sign. When I got out of jail the next morning, I left town. I had had hours to think about us. Your father was right. We were too different. You had dreams of going to college. I just wanted to earn a living."

Her father had connections in Hope, but would the former police chief do that? Either way, her father had been right that she and Zane weren't meant to be together. "So without talking to me, you gave up on us?" Knowing he hadn't accepted the money should have made her happy, but it didn't. What was wrong with her that men she was with wanted to leave her? First it was Zane, then later it was her husband.

"It wouldn't have changed my mind. When I left Hope, I hadn't intended to ever come back. We were young. We didn't know what we wanted."

I wanted you. She held those words inside. She would never tell him that. The past years had taken care of those feelings she'd had at eighteen. Instead she said, "The bottom line is I need your help with this house. At the very least I need a roof put on as quickly as possible. I want this to work. As far as I'm concerned, just as you said upstairs, what happened years ago is in the past. I'm not concerned about that. It's the future that has me worried."

"But will your father accept me here?"

"He will. He has to. He wants this house put back together. That's part of the reason he's so stressed. We're living in half the upstairs. We had to move our kitchen upstairs and make do with what we could rig up. Not the most ideal situation."

"Then I'll be here at two tomorrow. Can you give me the information about what shingles you want?"

"Yes. I've got it inside."

"I can make some calls and put a rush

on the delivery. In the meantime, I'll prep the roof, so as soon as the shingles are delivered, I can start on it. I should be able to pull another man from one of my other projects for a few days."

"My offer still stands. I will assist any way I can."

"For this part, there isn't much you can do except clean up the yard. That will save me some time."

"We can do that."

He moved up to the top step, his face coming more into the light streaming from the house. For a second, his medium-length black hair caught her attention. It still curled on his nape. She used to run her fingers through it and play with those curls. She wrenched her gaze away only to be snagged by his penetrating blue eyes. She used to think that was his best feature, but then he gave her his dazzling grin that took over his whole face and she'd decided it was his smile that appealed to her the most. But she hadn't seen that in years— the one where his two dimples appeared and his eyes shone with a rich brilliance. She missed it.

"I'm sorry to hear about your father's illness. He was never my favorite person, but I didn't want to see him sick."

His husky Southern drawl flowed over her, drawing her back into the past and threatening to melt her heart. She backed away a few feet and inhaled a deep breath, then another. "When Mom died, it wasn't long before he began to have problems. He went to the doctor, and they diagnosed him with Parkinson's disease, stage one. Now he's in stage two."

"Until I returned to Hope, I didn't realize your mother had died. What happened?"

"Stroke. She went quickly, but it was such a shock to Dad and me. She hadn't had any problems before that—at least ones we knew about. She had a way of not wanting to worry Dad with anything."

"She was a classy lady."

"Yeah. I still miss her."

"I know you two were close. I'm so sorry she's gone."

How was she going to keep her distance? The conversation was becoming personal. Zane knew so much about her from the year they had dated. But then she wasn't that person anymore, and from what she was glimpsing with him, he wasn't the same, either.

"Yes, we were close. She was not only my mother but my best friend." Her mom was the one who had helped her get through Zane leaving her. Her throat closing and tears threatening, Kim swung around and started for the door. She'd spent too much time revisiting the past today. She swallowed several times and said, "Let me find the information you need. Will you need any money up front?"

"No, we'll settle at the end."

"But what about the shingles?"

"Kim, you can pay everything—even the supplies—at the end. And I'll only charge you my costs. I'm trying not to make money on the tragedy that happened to Hope. That is the least I can do. The Lord has been good to me. I can afford it."

"Some people don't feel that way. Like the contractor we hired." She gave him a smile. "I'll be right back."

She went inside and up to her room and searched the top of her messy desk. When she found the shingle brochure, she made her way to the veranda, feeling for the first time in a long while a sense of hope. Her gaze skimmed over the heavy plastic sheeting hanging down and forming a corridor from the staircase to the front door. What happened to her home had stressed her more than she'd realized. Until the contractor had left town, she'd been able to suppress her concerns and feelings about the dishevelment her life had become. But not anymore.

Out on the veranda, she handed Zane the pamphlet with her notes on it. "We're still trying to settle with the insurance company, but the roof was covered fortunately. Once it's completely done they will pay us the rest of the money." She hoped it would pay for the supplies.

"I'll get on this right away. I'd better go. I need to go by the school and see how that project is wrapping up."

"So much of the original building was damaged beyond repair. I went to class there when I was in elementary school. I've been watching the changes you've had to make."

"Yeah, but it should retain a lot of its original architecture. Does it feel strange teaching where you went to school?"

She chuckled. "For the first few months, it did."

"There is a good side to this. The building is being updated. Some of the wiring and plumbing was old."

"I can't wait to get back into my own classroom. Right now we're at the rec center. The gym has been partitioned into different classes, but the noise level is so loud it can be distracting to students."

"I'm still surprised you're a teacher."

"At eighteen I didn't know what I wanted

to do other than to go to college." When she and Zane started getting serious, the idea of going to college had changed. She'd begun to see herself getting married and having three or four children— or doing both. Her life certainly didn't turn out as she'd planned. Although she still would love to have more children, that required a husband. She was through being emotionally vulnerable to a man. She would content herself with Anna and the kids in her class. "Teaching has allowed me to work with children. That's something I've enjoyed."

"From what I hear you're very good."

"Who did you hear that from?" The idea he had been talking about her to someone didn't bother her as much as it would have yesterday. Their talk this evening helped to clear the air some. When she got right down to it, she and Zane were worlds apart, and any marriage between them fifteen years ago wouldn't have lasted. He had been wise enough to see that. Back then she had believed love could overcome anything. Now reality had shown her how wrong that thinking was.

"My neighbor's son, Eric. He talks about you a lot. He told me you make learning fun."

"Did he just say that out of the blue?"

"No, we were talking about me fixing his school. He wanted to help. He hates having class at the rec center. He told me he has a hard time concentrating because of the noise. One thing led to another, and we ended up talking about you."

She blushed. Suddenly she felt thrust back to when she was a teenager and had a crush on Zane, who was a year ahead of her in school. Then he'd begun paying attention to her. "Will you have it ready for the grand opening?"

"One way or another. I have flood-lights for the night work on the outside that needs to be done. Most of what has to be finished, though, is inside work so I'm working two crews to get everything completed in time."

"I'd better let you go, then. I'll be so

happy when I'm back in my own class-room." She fluttered her hand in the air. "So go. Oversee or whatever you do."

He dipped his head forward slightly then descended the steps. Kim watched him as he got into his truck. When he glanced toward her, she waved and hurriedly turned away, the blush on her face intensifying. She loved observing people, but the last thing she wanted was to make him think she was interested by staring at him as he left.

After entering her house, she closed the front door, locked it and headed upstairs. She needed to check on her dad before she went to the room she shared with Maggie and Anna and crashed. What a day. She'd woken up to the news that her contractor had skipped out on her, and the day hadn't improved until Zane had finally agreed to help her. Although that arrangement presented a whole new set of problems— ones she wasn't sure she was prepared to handle.

Kim popped into her temporary bedroom to see if Anna was getting ready for bed. Her daughter was already under the covers while she read a book.

Anna set the book on her lap and smiled. "I like Mr. Davidson."

"I do, too," Kim admitted. More than she should.

"I'm not tired one bit. I'm gonna read awhile longer."

"That's fine. I've got to talk to Papa Keith." Kim leaned forward and kissed Anna on the cheek. "That's in case you fall asleep before I get back in here."

Anna returned her full attention to her book.

Kim quietly left her daughter reading a mystery, her first love when it came to literature.

When she saw Brady in the hallway, she stopped and asked, "Can you wait until I have a word with Dad?" Her father and Brady sharing a room wasn't an easy arrangement, but it had to work for a while longer until they at least could move into the rest of the rooms upstairs.

"Sure. I'll be in the game room. Just let me know when you're through."

"Thanks," Kim said then knocked on her father's door.

"Come in," her dad called out.

Kim entered, surprised to find him sitting at his desk in the corner. "I half expected to find you already asleep."

"I'm tired but not sleepy. I gave up staring at the ceiling, trying to fall asleep."

"So what are you doing?"

"Trying to pay some bills." His hand trembled so badly he dropped the pen next to the checkbook and curled his fingers into a fist.

"I thought you agreed I needed to do that from now on."

He glared at her. "I made a few mistakes. That's all. I don't plan on doing that again." The shaking had subsided some but not totally.

"Dad, it gets you so upset. I don't mind doing it."

"Leave me something to do. It seems lately there's so little I can do."

Kim crossed the room and sat in the chair near the desk, taking her father's hands and holding them. "Maggie would appreciate your help with the garden. You used to love to grow vegetables and flowers. Between you and the gardener, we had the best yard for miles around. We'd have people come by just to see your azaleas in bloom."

"And look at the bushes now. Most of them didn't make it through the storm. Only the ones at the back of the property where the water didn't flood."

"This spring would be a great time to plant some flowers."

He gestured toward the stack of bills. "With what money?"

"A teacher at my school has cuttings and bulbs she often shares with us in the spring. I could get some of those. And we don't know what will come back up. We had tulips and daffodils. They may bloom."

Her dad snorted and began working on the bills. "We'll see."

"Zane is going to be back tomorrow at two to start on the roof. He's going to complete the job Mr. Henderson—"

Tossing down the pen again, her father pushed back his chair and struggled to stand, tremors attacking his limbs. "I know you have it all set up, but that's what we nccd to talk about."

"Zane gave me a good deal. We don't have much money left to make the repairs since—"

"No!" His anger grooved his face in deep lines, making her father appear even older than he was.

Fortifying herself with a calming breath, Kim rose and reached out toward her dad.

He jerked away and put several feet between them. "I realize I should never have hired Henderson, but…" His words stumbled to a halt.

Her father had found Mr. Henderson and contracted him before Kim could have done much about it—all because she had mentioned approaching Zane's company to repair their house a month ago. In spite of their past, she'd known he was the best man for the job and from all she'd heard very reasonable.

"What's done is done. We need to move forward. At the very least, we have to get the roof taken care of. We can wait on the downstairs until we have enough money."

He pounded his fist into his palm. "I want my house back. Everything has been destroyed. Nothing is the same anymore." For the second time since the hurricane, tears filled his eyes. "I've lost so much. I feel useless to change it."

Kim moved closer, prepared for her dad to reject her attempt to comfort him. But as the tears trailed down his cheeks, he let her take him into her embrace and hug him, which, she realized, only emphasized the depth of his despair. "We're all doing what we can, Dad, including you. The storm surge on Hurricane Naomi was the worst to hit here for the past century."

"I dropped the flood insurance because we'd never had water problems and it cost so much on top of everything else. I'm to blame for the situation we're in. I've let the family down."

"No, you haven't. You've held us together for years. Now it's my turn." She leaned back and stared into his shiny eyes. "I need you to accept that Zane will be here helping us. Please, Dad. If we don't get the roof fixed, we will be in worse trouble."

Looking across the room, he cleared his throat. "I'll stay away."

"You won't give me any problems?"

He shook his head.

"You'll be civil to him?"

The twitching muscles in his jaw attested to the battle raging inside her father. "Yes" was his clipped response.

She rose up on her tiptoes and kissed her dad on the cheek. "Thank you. You'll see in a few months things are going to look brighter. The house is completely dried out and clean finally. We can work on restoring it as a family as time and money permits."

With his shoulders drooped, he made

his way to his bed and sat. "I'm tired. I'm going to try to sleep again."

"I'll let Brady know, so he's quiet when he comes in here." Kim exited her dad's bedroom and went toward the game room to find Brady.

He was sitting in an overstuffed chair at the opposite end from the temporary kitchen, playing a video game while Maggie knitted a prayer shawl in the recliner across from him.

Maggie looked up at her. "How's Uncle Keith?"

"He's gone to bed. Brady, he left the desk light on for you."

The twelve-year-old paused his game and stood. "Good night, Mom, Kim." As he walked from the kitchen, he resumed playing on his game console.

"Good thing Dad is a sound sleeper and Brady mutes the game."

Maggie laid the coral-colored shawl in her lap. "I was worried about that arrangement, but it has worked out. I think Brady and Uncle Keith have grown closer. Now if I can just get my son to stop teasing Anna, this might be a quiet house."

Exhaustion weighing her down, Kim sank into the chair Brady had vacated. "I feel better knowing that someone is in Dad's room with him."

"I thought with some time he would pull out of his depression, but he hasn't. Do you think he would talk to a counselor about what's been going on? Living through a hurricane can be a major trauma, especially for someone like Uncle Keith. The Christian Assistance Coalition has brought in a couple of counselors to help people deal with what has happened. They have some office space at city hall. When I go to work on Monday, I can check to see if there's anyone who could help Uncle Keith."

"If you can get me some information, I'll call them next week. The trick will be getting Dad to agree. He doesn't believe in that sort of stuff."

"You sound tired. Why don't you go

on to bed. I'll make sure everything is locked up."

Kim checked her watch. "To bed at nine o'clock on a Friday night. That about sums up my life. Dull and dateless."

Maggie's eyebrows lifted. "Is that remark because of Zane's visit tonight?"

"Partly. He certainly hasn't wanted for dates since he returned to Hope."

"Jealous?"

"No. Well, maybe a little. But my track record with men hasn't been good. Zane left me on my senior prom night. My husband left me because he preferred a marriage without children and promptly found himself one that fit his criterion."

"Scott doesn't count. He's a… There isn't a word to describe your ex-husband. How can a man leave a woman and a month-old baby?"

Kim laughed, but there was no amusement in the sound. "I think Dad was more shocked than I was. After all, he hand-picked Scott to be my husband."

"Yeah, and look what the man did."

"But he came from the right type of family, and he had a future."

"Running your family business into the ground."

Kim shivered. "Please don't remind me. We've never recovered from Scott being in our lives. But if it hadn't been for him, I wouldn't have Anna. She makes this all worth it."

Kim left the kitchen and started toward the bedroom she shared with Anna and Maggie, but in the hallway she paused at the top of the staircase. The faint light behind her spilled down the steps, dimly illuminating the darkness beyond. She saw some of the plastic sheeting, a constant reminder of the mess her life had become.

It seemed an eternity ago that she'd dreamed of being a wife and mother with at least three children. When she'd married Scott, she'd thought that dream had come true. Her father had thought Scott was perfect for her, and she'd even believed it for the first six months of their marriage. By the time he'd divorced her three and a half years later, she'd realized she'd married Scott on the rebound, a year after Zane had left. At nineteen she hadn't been ready to make that kind of commitment to another man—not after what had happened with Zane.

What would have happened if Zane and I had married?

Would her life have ended up in a disaster trying to hold her family together and keep the finances afloat?

Shaking her head, she turned away from the staircase, determined she would not let Zane disrupt her life. He was her past, and she'd declared tonight that she was going to move forward and look toward the future. That future did not include Zane.

Chapter Four

As Zane climbed down the extension ladder from the roof, Kim shielded her eyes and looked up. She finally had to glance away. Heights bothered her, and Zane was descending almost forty feet. "What's the verdict?"

"Most of the plywood has to be removed. It's old and rotten in a lot of places. I have to do that first before putting down the roofing felt and shingles."

"Mr. Henderson thought the plywood was fine except for a section over my bedroom where the tarp is."

With a few rungs remaining, Zane

jumped to the ground and landed in front of Kim. "He was wrong. That would have been a shortcut you would have noticed later when the roof started leaking. Sorry, but it will take longer than I thought before I inspected the roof more closely. I'm gonna need help to get this done before that storm system headed this way dumps a lot of rain on Hope."

Kim stepped back a couple of paces and looked all the way to the top of the house. "I can help you if you tell me what to do." Her words came out on a shaky thread that petered out at the end.

"I know a lot of things have changed over the past fifteen years, but I don't think your fear of heights is one of them."

She looked him square in the eye and straightened her posture. "I listened to the long-range forecast, and it is worse than I thought. They're predicting that big storm system moving through by Wednesday with gale-force winds. I can't afford not to help."

"I've got an idea of how to do it. Thankfully your roof isn't too steep. That makes it safer for the ones on it. I'm calling in a few favors and should be able to get some help over the next couple of days."

"Who?"

"Gideon, when his schedule permits. The same with Ian. How about your cousin, Colt?"

"Maybe. I can call him."

"I can also pull a couple of my men from the school if it looks like the storm will develop and hit us. That's still three days away. What the weatherman predicts doesn't always happen."

"What can I do?"

"Nothing right now. I'm gonna make some calls, get the supplies I need so I'll be ready to start first thing Monday morning."

"What about you working only in the afternoon? What about your other projects?" She didn't want to be beholden to him, but she needed the help.

"Can't a man change his mind?"

"Yes, but the school is supposed to open in three weeks."

"It will. I'll make it work."

Left unsaid but clear to Kim was the word *somehow*. She swallowed the tightness in her throat and said, "I need your help. I can't deny that. But maybe you need my help. If you're pulling men from the school project, let me do what I can there. I may not be able to do wiring, plumbing or a lot of the things you need done, but I can paint and do other types of finishing work."

"That's all right—"

"I insist you accept my help, and I'm sure Maggie will volunteer, too. She's taking Monday off because Brady will be home. If on that TV show they use volunteers to help build a house in a week, I'm sure you can find a need for both of us when it gets down to the wire with the school."

The smile—the one with his two dimples showing—lit his face, his eyes twinkling. "You haven't changed totally. You're still determined and persistent."

"I've had to be," she said then regretted it immediately. She didn't want to admit to him the past years had been hard for her after her husband walked out on her and Anna and almost totally ruined her family financially. It wasn't her way to air her dirty laundry for all to see. "So will you accept my help?"

He nodded. "If I need it." He started toward his truck. "I've got a lot to do if I'm going to get everything in place to start at first light Monday."

As he walked to his truck, Kim watched him, unable to take her eyes off him. This was not the person she had once known. What had changed him?

Anna ran around the side of the house. "Where's he going? I finished helping Maggie. I told him I could help him then."

"He's left for the day. He'll be back Monday morning."

"I wanted to help Zane."

"Zane?"

"He told me to call him that. Is that okay?"

"If he said so." She'd seen Anna talking with Zane when he'd come an hour ago, before he'd gone up on the roof. They had laughed about something then her daughter had raced around to the back where Maggie was finishing preparing the ground for the garden. For some reason, seeing Anna with Zane made Kim think of Scott. Her child had never really known her dad, and Kim had said little to her about him. But surely Anna wondered about the man who was her biological father. That was exactly how Kim had come to think of him— a biological father. About all he had contributed was his DNA.

She'd had such dreams of having a large family....

Releasing a long breath, Kim headed into the house to finish cleaning the rooms they lived in upstairs.

"Dad, I'm home," Zane called out as he entered his house later that day after securing the supplies and a couple of guys to help him Monday with Kim's roof.

"I'm in here."

Zane followed the sound of his dad's voice over the noise from the TV in the den. He found him out on the back deck, sitting in a lounge chair, smoking a cigarette in the dim light streaming from the bay window in the kitchen. Zane leaned against the wooden railing away from the drifting smoke. "How did your day go?"

"I finished working on the guest bathroom. Everything is back to the way it was before the hurricane."

"I appreciate it. I haven't had time to do anything on my own house."

His dad took a final puff on the cigarette and ground it into the coffee can he had on the deck. "I'm going to quit one day. Nasty habit."

"Dad, one step at a time. How was your AA meeting this afternoon?"

"Today is six months. As you said, one step at a time."

"I could use someone to help me with

the Sommerfield house. Do you think you can for the next couple of days?"

His father shot forward in the chair, all relaxation gone. "How can you work for that man?"

"I'm not. I'm working for Kim. She asked me to help her."

Both of his eyebrows rose. "She did? I'm sure her dad didn't send her."

"Nope."

"And you're going to work at his house?"

"Yup. When I left Hope years ago, I didn't do it the right way. I should have told Kim I was leaving. I owe her."

His dad bolted to his feet. "You don't owe that family nothing. Keith Sommerfield always felt he was better than everyone else."

"Dad, that's in the past."

"Is it?" He rotated toward the back door. "I have a feeling he didn't open his arms and welcome you to the family."

"Kim and I are in the past."

Going inside, his father muttered, "Are you?"

"Yes," Zane answered above the slamming door. Gripping the railing, he dropped his head and closed his eyes. The sound of a dog barking cut through the usual quiet on his piece of land outside of town in the middle of a pine forest, the scent of the trees wafting to him, carrying not one clue his home was only a few miles from the Gulf of Mexico.

In the past three months, he hadn't been at his house much except to sleep, making a mockery of why he lived on the outskirts of Hope. When he'd bought this acreage not long after he decided to stay in his hometown, he'd needed a place to escape from his memories of growing up in Hope. It hadn't been much of a haven lately.

He shoved away from the railing and covered the distance to the back door. In the kitchen, his dad was sticking a frozen dinner into the microwave.

"Want me to put one in for you?"

"No, I had dinner already. I thought you would have eaten by now."

"Wasn't hungry, but I've got to eat. You would think I'd throw myself into gaining weight. Food just doesn't interest me."

"There are a lot of people who would love to have that problem." His father's lanky body had taken a lot of abuse over the years he'd been drinking, to the point that it had begun to fail him. Going to his first AA meeting had been his dad's desperate attempt to do something about his health. "Do you want some company?"

"Only if you'll promise me you'll be careful at your new job. The Sommerfields treated you lousy years ago. Don't let them use you now."

When he'd returned home after being gone for a year, Zane had heard from his father nothing but how bad Keith Sommerfield, and for that matter Kim, had been to him. He'd stayed not quite a day and most of the time he'd spent fighting with his dad. Maybe it was better his father didn't help at the Sommerfield home. "On second thought I'm tired, and I have to get up early. See you tomorrow.

I'll be gone before you get up and probably won't come back until late."

Zane moved toward the hallway, but his dad stepped into his path before leaving the kitchen. "Son, you have been here for me when I needed someone to force me to get sober. I want you to know I'm here for you. Protect yourself."

"Sure." Zane skirted around him and quickened his pace out of the room.

Now his father was trying to be a parent—now when he didn't need him to be. He knew the turnaround was because his dad wasn't drinking. He'd finally sought help when the doctor told him he would die in under a year if he didn't do something about his lifestyle. Too much alcohol and unhealthy eating had taken their toll on his father's thin, frail body.

The man he'd finally persuaded to live with him six months ago had been a shell of a man. At least lately he was beginning to put some meat on his bones and regain his strength and stamina.

But that didn't change the fact Zane was

waiting for his father to slip and dive back into a bottle, leaving him to pick up the pieces…again.

"He's here."

Anna's declaration wrenched Kim from a deep sleep, and she bolted up in bed. She spied Anna by the window overlooking the front of the house, dressed as though she'd been up for hours. Kim glanced at the clock on the bedside table.

7:00 a.m.!

"I set the alarm for six. What happened?"

"You slept through it. We didn't wake you 'cuz Maggie thought you should get some more rest." Anna turned from the window with her hand on her waist. "Maggie's right. You haven't been sleeping well lately."

Her mind still fuzzy with sleep, Kim threw back the covers and climbed out of bed. She needed at least two or three cups of coffee before she faced Zane or for that matter dealt with her daughter, who had decided to switch roles and try her hand at parenting. "I'm fine. I got nine hours of sleep last night."

"Exactly. I'll let Maggie know you're up. She's making cinnamon rolls before I go over to Polly's." At the door, Anna peered over her shoulder. "I think I should stay and help you this morning."

"I saw you eyeing that ladder Saturday. You are *not* getting up on that roof or the ladder. I'll save the mess for you and Brady to clean up later. How about that?"

"Mom, you're always thinking of me."

"Young lady, sarcasm isn't becoming on you." But Anna was gone. Kim let out a huff and closed the door.

Several male voices drifted to her from the game room. Who else did Zane get to help? Her cousin hadn't been able to come today because he'd left to pick up a boat yesterday in Florida and bring it back to Hope.

Kim moved to the front window and peeked out at a Jeep, Zane's black truck and a white pickup. She hurried and dressed, pausing a moment in front of the mirror to look at her wild curls. Searching through her dresser, she finally found a ponytail holder to bring some kind of order to the mess. High humidity always did this to her hair. She wouldn't be surprised if it rained tomorrow instead of Wednesday as they predicted.

Then she made the mistake of looking down at her attire and winced. She'd dressed as if she was going to work as a teacher at school, forgetting that this Monday school wasn't in session. She quickly changed her nice slacks for jeans and donned tennis shoes instead of flats. Why was the prospect of spending the whole day with Zane muddling her brain?

Opening the door into the hallway, she inhaled a composing breath. She had to get used to the fact he would be in her life at least for a while. But the mere thought of that caused her heart to flutter, and all the composure she'd mustered vanished.

Until she entered the game room and saw Tom Davidson, Zane's father, standing next to his son. The memory of pleading with the man to tell her where Zane was the day after prom flashed before her. It kept her rooted in the entrance to the room.

Zane saw her and smiled a greeting. "Maggie insisted we come in for some breakfast and coffee. I couldn't say no after I got a whiff of the cinnamon rolls she baked."

The scent of them saturated the air, enticing people to forget their diet and taste one of them. "I keep telling her to quit her job for the mayor and open a bakery."

Maggie removed the baking sheet from the oven. "How about a bakery and a nursery? People could come for some goodies and buy a plant at the same time."

"That sounds like a plan. I'll be there." Zane picked up a mug, filled it and passed it to his dad. Then he repeated it until Gideon and Ian had theirs. His gaze skimmed to her. "Do you want any?"

The question she should have been asking everyone forced from her mind the surprise of seeing Zane's dad in her home. "Yes, please." She crossed to the counter to help Maggie set the rest of the food out—slices of pineapple, melon and oranges, as well as bagels with cream cheese.

Zane slid the mug toward Kim. "Here. We can't stay long. We have a lot to do today. I want to replace all the rotten ply-wood and put the roofing felt down. Then tomorrow and the next day I can get the shingles on before the storm hits Wednes-day night. And who knows, it might not happen."

"You're going to shingle by yourself?"

"Dad is gonna help me. He used to work as a roofer."

Kim stepped closer and lowered her voice. "I'm surprised he's here."

"Frankly, I am, too. When I first said something, he told me no, but this morn-ing he was up before me, ready to come help. Lots of stuff has been happening with him since he started AA." He cocked a grin. "I'm afraid to say too much about it. I don't want to jinx it."

"I'm glad to hear that," she murmured, trying to mean that. But she was still bothered by the fact that he had known where Zane was all those years ago and lied to her.

"I'm hoping this works out. I've been thinking lately about getting my dad involved in my business. Give him something to do. He lost his job at the fishery when the hurricane hit and destroyed the place. He's been helping some of his friends with their houses and businesses, but he needs something steady and permanent to keep him..." Zane peered over his shoulder.

Kim leaned toward him. "Sober?"

Zane nodded.

"Hey, you two, we're starved and you're standing in front of the food," Gideon said behind Kim and Zane.

Kim spun toward Gideon, who was holding a plate in his hand, tapping his foot with a huge grin on his face. "Where's

Kathleen? Did she finally come to her senses and flee Hope before the big day?"

"Funny, I keep wondering that myself. But she and her mother are gonna be over later."

"They are?"

"Yes, they're bringing lunch for all of us." Gideon snatched a cinnamon roll and put it on his plate.

"They don't have to do that. Maggie and I were going to make some sandwiches."

"They wanted to help, but I forbade Kathleen getting up on the roof to help. She's afraid of heights and had a tough time shutting the second-story shutters when the hurricane hit."

"I know the feeling." Kim sidled down the counter to give everyone room to get to the dishes.

"O'Brien, move along before you hog all the food." Ian McShane, the local police chief, edged his way in beside Gideon. "I require a lot of carbs to work."

Kim stepped toward Maggie while the

men filled their plates. "Where's Brady and Anna?"

"Gone to Polly's. They grabbed a bagel and rushed out of here. I'm glad they're going over there. Too many people underfoot might be too much for your dad."

"Yeah, I wish he'd come out, but I couldn't talk him into it, just like you couldn't yesterday for church. He'll probably stay in his room all day. I don't like that, but it would be better than him in the middle of everything."

"Your dad hasn't gone to church since your mom died." Maggie turned her back on the men and ushered Kim a few feet away. "For that matter, your attendance has dropped off, especially since the hurricane. You used to be so involved. What's going on?"

"Do I really have to tell you that? What has been going right lately? Nothing. I'm worried about Dad. I'm worried about our house. I'm worried about money and—"

"Kim, give your worry to the Lord. He

can handle it. Worry pulls us down until we become ineffective."

"How do you stop worrying when everything is literally falling apart around us?"

"Other than giving you added stress, what do you get from worrying? Has it taken care of the problem? Does all this worrying make you feel better?"

"That's easy for you to say but a whole lot different for me to stop. I've spent my life worrying."

"Yeah, I know. It's an ingrained habit that is disrupting your sleep until you are so exhausted that you don't hear an alarm going off right next to you."

"About that. You should have awakened me."

"You needed the sleep." Maggie would have continued her lecture, Kim knew, but Zane's dad called to her from the table where the men were eating.

"This is delicious. I think you should forget about the nursery and focus on the bakery."

Maggie smiled. "Thank you. A cook can never get too many compliments."

Kim went to the counter to get something to eat while silence fell over the room as the men ate. Maggie's advice still rang in her mind. Her logical side told her Maggie was right, but she didn't know how to stop from worrying.

Kim turned toward the table and halted. Her dad stood in the entrance, thunder on his face. He opened his mouth to say something, glared at her and snapped it close, then pivoted and left. She closed her eyes and wondered if anything would ever change. For sure now he would spend the rest of the day in his room, which at the moment might be for the best.

When she glanced toward the table, she caught Zane's gaze directed on her, a softness in his eyes that she hadn't ever seen. It connected with her, spoke to her. No, she would not fall for him again. He broke her heart once. She should never have married Scott and wouldn't have if

Zane hadn't left town. He abandoned her. She had to remember that.

She wrenched her attention from him and took the chair at the other end of the table from him, fisting her hands in her lap until they stopped trembling, much like her father often did.

"Kim, I've contacted the communities around here about Henderson, as well as the state police," Ian told her. "I'm hoping we can get the money back that he stole from y'all plus what it takes to repair correctly the other houses he did." He downed the rest of his coffee then got up to bring the carafe to the table.

"Thanks, I appreciate any help in getting our money back."

"I found out yesterday he skipped out on the Collins family, too, leaving the work half done. I hope you'll be able to help them, too, Zane." Ian refilled his mug.

"Yeah, when we finish with the school. What's the problem for them? Anything urgent?"

"No, just interior rooms. Nothing like the roof here, thankfully."

"Good. Then just have Will Collins contact me."

"The problem is that he lost some of his money to Henderson like Kim. He didn't have too much to begin with and now this." He took a sip of his coffee.

Zane's gaze pinned Kim's. "I'll work something out with him. When disaster hits an area, it hurts everyone, but especially the people who can't afford to rebuild."

"You're doing what you can for the town. I know Kathleen's neighbor, Miss Alice, was grateful for the help." Gideon rose and took his dishes to the sink. "I'm heading outside to unload my tools and the supplies you put in back of my Jeep."

"We're coming, too." Ian grabbed Zane's dad's plate and stacked it on his, then carried both to the counter.

"I'll take Uncle Keith something to eat," Maggie told Kim. "You'd better stay here and give him time to cool off." She loaded food onto a dish and hurried out of the kitchen.

Her stomach clenched, Kim studied her half-eaten roll, dreading what Zane would say after Maggie's reference to her father.

"I thought your dad was going to be all right about me being here."

She gripped her fork and stabbed a piece of pineapple. "He said he would be." She lifted her head. "He doesn't have a say in this. I'll try and keep him away."

"That's fine. After my father's reaction the other night, I understand. Maybe we should leave them in a room to duke it out, since they both have problems with us even talking with each other."

With her hands cupped around the warm mug, she raised it to her lips and sipped the coffee, its aroma mingling with the cinnamon. "Neither one has changed much in fifteen years. When I talked with him after you left, Dad made it clear that he was glad you left to avoid marrying me. He said we weren't meant to be together."

"He was right." Zane came to his feet, brought his dishes to the sink and started for the outside door to the upstairs gallery. "I have to go. I can't stay in here and talk about why it didn't work for us when I'm the one who asked the guys to come help me. I need to be out there doing my share."

"I'll be coming— "

The sound of the door shutting cut off the rest of her words. Friday night she'd felt they had taken a step forward. Just now they'd taken two steps back. And she realized she didn't want it that way. Once, they had shared a friendship, as well as love. She wanted that friendship back, but she didn't think Zane felt the same way.

Chapter Five

"It looks like they're making good progress," Kathleen Hart said as she climbed from her car in front of Kim's family home.

"They're about halfway done with the plywood and roofing felt." Kim followed Kathleen, Gideon's fiancée, to the trunk of her vehicle. "You didn't have to do this. We'd planned to feed everyone."

"I know. But I wanted to. I figured you had enough to cope with." She pointed to the mess that littered the yard, then popped the trunk.

"It wasn't too bad until they started on

the roof that needed the old shingles removed. I've only had a couple of minor leaks on the middle section. Nothing like the right or left side of the second floor."

Kathleen handed Kim a large, clear plastic container with sandwiches. "It'll be nice when you're completely dry."

"Yeah, since the hurricane, every time it's rained, I've found another water spot on the ceiling."

"Mom had that problem over the garage and kitchen."

"Speaking of Ruth, how's the campaign for mayor going?" Kim headed for the two card tables she'd brought out for the food. Recently, Ruth Coleman had decided to run for mayor after the current one pressured Kathleen's mother to run for the office.

"I'm seeing a whole new side to my mom. She has dived into this with both feet."

"She's a shoo-in with the our mayor now endorsing her."

Kathleen unloaded a paper sack with

chips, brownies and a vegetable tray. "I don't know. Her opponent has some big money behind him."

"He hasn't lived here very long. Money isn't everything when running for office."

Setting the jug of iced tea down next to the paper cups, Kathleen scanned the area. "Where's Maggie?"

"She went to get some chocolate-chip cookies she made."

"Good. I want to hear her take on this race since she works for the mayor."

"Ruth's got her vote and mine."

Kathleen laughed. "I can't believe I've turned into my mom's unofficial campaign manager at the same time I'm planning my wedding."

"And working at the hospital."

"Don't forget my two active boys. I need to find someone to help her besides me."

"Why didn't they come with you? Anna and Brady are inside, but they'll be out here soon." Kim stepped toward the front of the house where the guys were working, cupped her hands around her mouth and shouted, "Time to eat."

Zane stuck his head over the edge of the roof. "Great. We'll be down as soon as we finish one area."

"Don't wait too long. I see Anna and Brady coming down the staircase."

The partially open double doors flew wide as both children burst from the house, dressed in jeans and T-shirts, with Maggie right behind them.

Her daughter skidded to a halt a few inches shy of one of the tables. "I'm starved."

Kim released her captured breath slowly and said, "When aren't you hungry?"

Anna grinned. "When I'm asleep."

Brady reached for a paper plate and snagged two sandwiches from the plastic container in time for Maggie to say, "Haven't you heard of taking one sandwich at a time? You'd better eat both of them."

"Mom, that's not gonna be hard. Now,

four might be a *real* challenge." He started to pick up another one.

Maggie swatted his hand. "Don't even think that. Give the guys who have been working a chance to get their lunch."

"I'm gonna be working after lunch. Look." He nodded toward the debris from the roof, mostly old shingles and pieces of damaged plywood. "Me and Anna gotta clean up the yard. We need fuel for that."

"Yeah, Mom. Fuel." Anna piled her plate with extra chips and even a few carrots and celery sticks.

As Brady and Anna strolled to the steps of the house, Maggie placed the cookies next to the brownies. "I checked on Uncle Keith. He's sitting in his room, watching TV. He grunted at me and kept his attention on some sporting event. But I doubt he even knew who was playing."

"I'm sure you're right. Dad isn't much into sports."

Maggie looked around. "Where are Kip and Jared? Brady was hoping they would come and help him with cleaning up."

"Making placards for Mom's campaign. She and Miss Alice are printing the slogan on the poster, and my sons are hammering them to the stakes. A nice production line." Kathleen's eyes lit up when Gideon strode toward her and kissed her. As the rest of the men approached, she said, "There are tuna-fish and chicken-salad sandwiches."

"Now you know why I'm marrying this lady in four weeks. She makes the best chicken salad." Gideon gave Kathleen a plate. "After you."

Kim stood back and observed the couple—the looks exchanged, the touches shared—and her heartbeat slowed. She'd wanted that at one time. She'd had it with Zane, even with Scott. But not for long. She rotated away, facing the direction of the Gulf. She glimpsed the blue sparkling water through the pine and live oaks still remaining after the hurricane that had taken over a third of them.

Zane lowered his head toward her, his breath fanning her neck. "You okay?"

She shivered. Angling toward him at the same time she took a step back, she glimpsed the worry in his gaze. "I'm fine. Thinking about old times."

"When we were dating?"

She nodded, her throat jamming with emotions she'd thought she had rid herself of over the years. "Among other things. You are part of my past."

"Do you see us being friends in the future?"

The question threw her off guard. "I—I…"

"I know it's over between us, but I used to enjoy your company. Seeing you again, talking with you, has made me realize that."

"Well, yes. I guess so."

One corner of his mouth tilted upward. "I love how you say that with such enthusiasm. Good for my ego."

She shook off her apprehension and said in a strong voice, "Of course, we can be friends."

"That's much better." He held out his

hand. "C'mon. Let's go eat before there's nothing left for us."

She fit her palm against his, a spark sending an electrifying streak up her arm. She almost pulled her hand away but didn't. Zane was putting his work on hold because of her. The least she could be was civil to him—a friend as he said. But no more than that. Her fragile composure wouldn't survive it.

Zane passed her a paper plate. "Is your dad gonna eat?"

"I'll take him something after we finish."

"Then you'd better set his aside now. I see Brady heading back for thirds."

"I already did." Maggie sat nearby in one of the folding chairs she and Kim had brought out earlier. "I put it just inside the front door. I figured you'd want to take it up to him later."

"Thanks. It's probably a good thing he isn't out here." Kim peered toward the house, half expecting her father to appear and demand everyone leave.

"So he really isn't okay with all of this?" Zane took a seat next to Maggie.

"His way of coping is to hide in his room. I've seen my dad's health decline over the last few months since the hurricane. I'm hoping getting his place fixed will help him, but I'm not even sure if that will."

"I've gotten to know Cody Weston at church. He has a doctorate in psychology. He's working as a counselor with the Christian Assistance Coalition. He's seeing that a lot with the townspeople. It's not unusual in these kinds of circumstances. Do you think your dad would talk to him?" Zane asked as he bit into his sandwich.

"I don't know. Maybe if he knew the man first. He's pretty reserved with strangers."

Maggie leaned around Zane. "That's the group I was gonna talk to tomorrow. If you know someone, that's even better."

"But how do we get Dad to meet Cody?

He doesn't leave the house lately unless he needs to go to the doctor's."

Zane snared Kim's attention. "Then we'll bring Cody here."

His look conveyed she wasn't alone, that he would help her with her father, as well as the house. "How?"

"I think I have an idea," Kathleen said across from them. "Your dad and my mom are friends. Let's have a campaign meeting here. We need calls and signs made. A planning session."

"That doesn't mean Dad will participate."

"If he balks at doing it, I'll sic Mom on him. He could never say no to her. I don't know what I'm doing. Something like a political campaign isn't my expertise."

An idea weaved its way into Kim's thoughts. Her dad had worked on a few campaigns for his friends in the past. "When do you want to do it, Kathleen?"

"We have a meeting set up for Thursday evening. Is that okay with you?"

Kim wasn't sure how this would work,

but she hoped it did. Her dad couldn't go on the way he was and decline even more. "Yes, and thanks, Kathleen." She shifted her attention to Zane. "Can you come and bring Cody?"

"I can, but am I the best one to do it? Your dad doesn't want me here."

"As I said earlier, Dad needs to get used to you being here if you're going to be repairing the roof." And besides, his presence helped her. Zane had taken his life and made something of it. He was strong—in body, mind and faith. She needed that right now, even if she wouldn't admit it to him.

His visual survey of her face heightened her awareness of him even more. Her pulse reacted by picking up speed. She pushed to her feet. "I'd better go take Dad his lunch. If you aren't here when I get back, Kathleen, thanks again for this delicious spread of food. I'm going to have to get you and Maggie to teach me how to cook better."

Kathleen grinned. "Anytime. And I'll call you to arrange Thursday night."

Kim cut across the yard toward the veranda. Out of the corner of her eye, she spied Zane's dad watching her. A frown, directed at her, marred his leathered features. She focused forward and mounted the steps, then crossed to the front door. Inside, she took her father's plate up to his room, knocked then entered because the television was up so loud she doubted he could hear her rap.

"At least the racket has calmed down for now. Are they finished?" he asked over the blare of the cheering crowd at some basketball game.

"No, Dad." She placed the plate on the table beside his chair in front of the TV, then turned the sound down and sat across from him. "Kathleen, Ruth's daughter, made the food. I especially like the chicken salad."

His gaze glued to the game on the screen, he huffed. "Why did she do it?"

"Gideon is helping, so I guess she thought she would, too."

"We don't need all this help. We can get along just fine without—"

"Hold it right there. We do need the help. I know it. You know it. And in exchange we're going to help Kathleen and Ruth. Thursday I'm hosting a campaign-strategy party here at the house. Ruth's running for mayor, and we're going to help her. She would be great running Hope."

"She shouldn't have any trouble winning, so why the worry?"

"Her opponent has a lot of money behind him. Ruth is conducting a grassroots campaign, which needs people. We're going to be some of those people."

"Me? What can I do?" He held out his shaking hand.

"Do you think Ruth would make a good mayor?"

"Yes."

"Then you can help with all the people you know in Hope." She rose as the nail gun started again above them. "I expect you to be at the meeting. If you don't want to be beholden to others then you have to give back. Thursday is a good start."

When she took a step toward the door, her father turned the TV sound up to its previous loud volume.

Her head pounded as the noise bombarded her from two sides. Kim shut the door and leaned against it. Although the TV's blare was muted some, her head still ached. Massaging her fingertips against her temples, she prayed Thursday would work.

Night inched closer, the dim light too weak to do any more work on the roof. Zane descended the ladder last and laid it on its side against the house in the backyard. He peered up at the door to the game room from the upstairs gallery. "I'm telling Kim we're leaving, Dad, then we can go and get something to eat."

"I've seen you looking at her today. Don't get involved with her again. She isn't right for you. Don't let her use you."

Zane gritted his teeth but couldn't *not* reply to his father. "Use me? That isn't the type of person Kim is."

"Are you so sure about that? You're a wealthy man now." His dad swept his arm across his body. "Who better to put this place back to its former glory."

"You think you have to stand up for me. Don't. I can take care of myself."

"A slur against you is a slur against me."

"Is that what this is about?"

His dad narrowed his eyes. "I know what people think about me. I'm trying to change, yet it's people like Kim's dad who still give me looks like I'm a leper."

He closed the space between his father and him. "Give them time. They'll see you're staying sober. You're strong. You can do it."

"You don't really believe that." He pushed past Zane and stalked toward the truck.

Lord, how do I help my dad? I don't want to lose him again to alcohol. Please show me the way.

He mounted the stairs to the second-floor gallery and knocked on the door to the game room. Perched on the roof, he'd seen Kim down below helping Brady and Anna pick up the scraps. Once she'd looked up as he had been staring at her. He should have gone right back to work, but he couldn't take his eyes off of her. She smiled at him and waved before her daughter said something to her and Kim peered away. But her smile had stayed with him for hours as he put the roofing felt down.

She opened the door, and again he found himself trapped by her look, words fleeing his mind. Her eyes gleamed first, and then the corners of her mouth lifted. A warmth spread through his chest to encompass his whole body even though the night had turned the breeze cold.

"Hi. Did you need anything?" she finally asked.

He cleared his dry throat. "Just wanted to let you know I'll be back tomorrow afternoon after lunch to start on the shingles. I'm gonna bring one of my workers to help me. We should have the whole roof done by late Wednesday afternoon before the storm."

"Great."

He didn't move—couldn't.

She glanced over his shoulder. "Where's your dad?"

"Cooling off in the truck, which is why I'm not too eager to join him at the moment."

"Y'all have a fight?"

"I'm thirty-four, and he's trying to tell me how to live my life. This from a man who has spent most of his time drinking and in a alcohol haze a good part of his life." He breathed in the scents of jasmine and cooking meat. "Smells good."

"Maggie is fixing a roast chicken. Would you like to eat dinner with us?" She paused for a few seconds before adding, "Your dad can, too, if he wants."

"No. We'll grab something on the way home. But I'll take a glass of water."

"Sure." She stepped to the side. "Come in. I'll get it for you."

He'd give his dad another couple of minutes before he joined him. Right now he wasn't sure what he would say to him if he started in again about Kim and her father.

When she filled a glass and gave it to him, his fingers grazed hers. He nearly dropped the drink but covered his reaction to her touch by quickly raising it to his lips and sipping the water.

"Kim, where are you?" her father shouted right before he came into the game room. His glance strayed to Zane then Kim. "They've revised the weather forecast. It looks like the storm system will be here a day early. It's really building up west of us. It doesn't look good for us, especially with gale-force winds."

"That means a tarp probably wouldn't be enough to protect our house." Kim threw an appealing gaze toward Zane.

"Then we have to get all the shingles on tomorrow. They're delivering them by eleven, but it'll be faster if I pick them up myself. If I have to, I'll work on the roof after dark. I've got some floodlights I can use. Tomorrow night you'll have your new roof." Zane took another swig of the water, then put the glass on the counter. "I'll be here after I get the shingles. I'll pull as many workers as I can spare from the school to help me." He strolled toward the outside door. He knew the owner of the supply house. He'd try him this evening. Maybe the man could open up earlier tomorrow so he could get the shingles sooner.

Kim followed him to the door. "Thank you. Are you sure you can afford to use your men?"

"I have to. There are a couple of other places we're working that will need the same kind of attention. You aren't the only one I'll have to pull men from the school for." He clasped her hands. "Don't worry. I'm not gonna let anything happen to this house."

"I appreciate it. I'm not sure how much more Dad can take."

The worry and pain he glimpsed in her eyes prompted him to cup her face. "Is he the only one you're worried about?"

"Yes." Her eyes glistened. "I'm fine." She backed away. "See you tomorrow."

He left Kim's and headed for the side of the house where his truck was parked. When he rounded the corner, he stumbled to a halt. His truck was gone. What did his father do?

In the past, his dad had done impulsive things when he was upset and they usually led to him drinking. He looked back toward the lights in the game room, then tried his dad's cell. It went to voice mail. He left a message but knew his father wouldn't be calling him anytime soon. After trudging back up the stairs, he knocked again on the door.

When Kim appeared in the entrance, she frowned. "What's wrong?"

"I need a ride home."

"What's wrong with your truck?"

"It's gone. I guess Dad got tired of waiting."

She chuckled. "So he left you to walk home."

He gave her a grin. "Not if a pretty lady will give me a ride home."

"Then do you want me to get Maggie for you?"

For a few seconds, he didn't know what to say to that. Then he saw her smirk and answered, "I guess I can settle for you."

She planted her hand on her waist. "I hope you have on some good walking shoes."

He peered down at his work boots, then up at her. "Well, yeah, but I've been working all day, and I'm just plumb tired. Can you help me? Please."

"Come in. I'll get my purse. Do you want to stay for dinner before going home?"

He started to say yes, but the word clogged his throat. Instead he shook his head. "Thanks. Another time." He stayed out on the gallery, but through the open door, he spied the family taking their seats at the table. He didn't know what that feeling was like to have a family sitting around a table talking, sharing dinner. Even now with his dad living with him, they rarely ate a meal together.

When Kim came back, Zane said, "I'm sorry about taking you away from dinner, but—" he lowered his voice "—I'm worried about Dad. He might have been angrier than I thought. I didn't think he would drive away and leave me."

She shut the door behind her. "I love chicken, hot or cold. I'll be fine. Besides, it won't take me that long."

In the car, Kim switched on the engine and pulled out of her long driveway onto the highway that ran along the coast. Two blocks away, she turned right and headed away from the Gulf toward the area Zane directed her to. "The area where you live is newly developed. How did it weather the hurricane?"

"Not too bad since we're about four miles from the Gulf. My home backs up to Lake Hope."

"Do you see many alligators around your place?"

"Two in the last couple of years."

"Don't tell Anna. She'd want to come to your house and keep watch for one."

Picturing Kim's inquisitive daughter brought a smile to his lips. Every time he'd come down to the ground today, she'd been right there asking questions about the roofing process. "I'll remember that."

Ten minutes later, Kim parked in front of Zane's dark house. "It looks empty."

"Yeah. That worries me."

"What did you two fight about?"

The irony of this conversation struck him. "My father doesn't approve of me helping you."

"Then why did he come and help today?"

He didn't need to see her face in the dark to know that Kim was hurt. It laced each word and made him wish he hadn't said anything. But he wasn't going to lie to her. "He knew I needed everyone I could get today. Lately he's been doing some odd jobs around here and in the neighborhood. I'm hoping he's getting back into the routine of working. For a long time, his drinking kept him from having a job for long."

"I guess you were right. We should put our two dads in a locked room and let them duke it out. My dad doesn't want you in my life, and yours feels the same way about me. I don't understand them making such a big deal out of it. We're only friends now."

"Yeah, friends. I guess they don't even want that."

"Tough. I have to be able to live my own life, and Dad is going to have to realize that."

"Right. I told mine that."

Kim shifted toward him, her fragrance of jasmine permeating every part of the interior. "Go check and see if he's here. If he isn't and you want to find him, I'll take you."

"You would?"

She clasped his arm nearest her. "Yes.

And if you want, I can even talk to your father. Assure him my intentions are honorable."

He burst out laughing. "Sounds like we're living a hundred years ago and our roles are reversed."

"I love your laugh. I can remember that time you laughed so hard when I fell into my cousin's pool fully clothed."

"I know I shouldn't have, but you should have seen your face. You couldn't believe that little boy pushed you."

"It certainly made me reconsider babysitting a relative. I didn't even get paid for looking like a fool in front of everyone."

"Not to me. You were adorable. An adorable drowned rat—I mean cute little dog."

Facing forward, she started the car. "I'm not sure being referred to as a drowned dog is much better than a drowned rat."

"Oh, yes, much better. I'll be right back." Zane hopped from the car and hurried into his house. A minute later, he was back. His worry mingling with a frown implied his dad wasn't home even before he slid back onto the front seat. "Let's go down Highway 90 and check the bars."

"You think he'll begin drinking again?"

"I hope not. His liver won't last much longer if he does. But I've got to check those places in Hope first."

"What if you don't find him there?"

"Then I'll have you take me home, and I'll wait for him after I call Ian. His men can be on the lookout for my truck."

"It helps knowing the police chief," Kim said, coming to a four-way stop on Gator Road.

"I could have used that fifteen years ago."

Before putting her foot on the accelerator, she threw him a glance. "Do you think my dad was responsible for you being arrested prom night?"

"Only he can tell you that. Even if he was, it's not important now."

"Yeah, but if he did, that was so wrong of him. He shouldn't think he can—"

"Kim, don't. It's the past. I meant it

when I told you I have forgiven your father for what happened all those years ago."

"How can you?"

"Because it takes too much energy to keep up that kind of anger. When I left Hope, I didn't feel that way. Even when I lived here, I was an angry guy."

At a stoplight on Highway 90, Kim tapped her fingers against the steering wheel. "You're a changed man?"

"Yeah, getting to know the Lord can do that to you."

"Maybe." The light switched to green, and Kim pressed her foot down on the accelerator, shooting across the intersection.

"Slow down a little. There are a few bars he used to frequent along this strip."

Silence descended for the next few minutes as Zane searched the parking lot of every bar they passed—until they came to the last one before leaving the city limits.

"He's there." Zane pointed toward his black truck parked boldly in front of the bar.

Chapter Six

"Thank you. I can take it from here." Zane opened the passenger door and put one foot down on the ground.

The light from the bar's neon sign shone on his face, revealing deep lines of sadness etched into his features. "Will you be all right?" Kim asked.

"Sure. It's not like I haven't gone after my father before and brought him home drunk."

Her heart wrenched at his words. She didn't want him to be alone. It was hard enough dealing with an alcoholic but doing it by yourself was doubly difficult. She opened her door.

As she rose and peered over the top of her car, his gaze met hers. "No. A bar isn't a place for you, especially this one. Why do you think it's on the outskirts of town?"

"I'm going in with you. Otherwise, I would be left sitting by myself waiting in the car. That doesn't sound too safe, either."

"How about driving away? I'll even wait to go in until you've left."

"Nope. You aren't alone this time dealing with your dad. I'm here. Just as you have been these past few days for me. I won't be able to leave until I know how your dad is."

He stared at her for a long moment then pivoted toward the entrance. "Suit yourself. I warned you."

Kim scurried after Zane into the bar, a wall of smoke blasting her in the face. She blinked her stinging eyes. How could anyone sit in here and drink?

As blaring music from a jukebox played, Zane paused and took stock of the place.

The bartender saw him and gestured toward a booth in the back on the right. Zane swung his gaze toward it and stiffened.

Kim glimpsed the top of his dad's head, the light from above shining on his bald spot as he bent over the table, his chin resting on his upper torso. Zane reached back and grabbed her hand, then moved in between the tables until he stopped at the last booth.

His dad slowly raised his head. Tears filled the older man's eyes, the same dark blue as Zane's. "What are you doing here?" he asked in a voice full of anger.

"Taking you home." Zane touched his father's arm.

He jerked it away. "I don't wanna go. I might not drink this." He waved his hand at a small glass with a dark liquor in it. "Then again I might. It's *my* decision. Not yours."

Zane slipped into the booth across from his dad and tugged Kim down next to him. "Then we'll stay here and keep you company," he said over the loud music playing in the background. "Staying here may be your decision, but driving my truck home isn't."

The old man straightened, fastening his intense regard on Kim. "What's she doing here?"

"She gave me a ride and wanted to make sure you were okay."

"Yeah, I'm sure she cares."

Kim held his look. "I do care. You're Zane's father. You helped me when I needed it today."

"I remember what you said to me when I wouldn't tell you where Zane was." Mr. Davidson tapped the side of his head. "I don't forget those kinda things."

"Dad, that was—"

"I don't care. She told me to go drown myself in a bottle."

Zane shot her a look.

"I did, but I was upset and hurting. I said some things I've regretted. I've wanted to apologize to you." That was the only thing she could do when she saw the pain on the man's face as he struggled with his addiction.

Mr. Davidson tilted up his chin. "What's stopping you?"

"Nothing. I'm sorry for what I said. It was wrong. Please accept my apologies."

"Nope. I won't." Zane's dad clasped the glass in front of him, and slowly with hands trembling he brought the liquor toward his mouth.

Zane tensed. His hand clenched.

When the drink reached Mr. Davidson's lips, Zane knocked it from the man's grasp. "No, don't do it. It's killing you."

The glass shattered against the floor. Drops splattered on Kim's jeans.

The older man scrambled from the booth. "Get out of here. I don't need a keeper. I'll do what I want," he shouted, drawing everyone's attention in the bar. He swiveled around and stormed to the counter to order another drink.

"I shouldn't have done that."

"If he doesn't want to change and stop drinking, nothing you do will change that." Kim slid out of the booth followed by Zane.

"I know, but I can make sure he doesn't drink and drive." Zane marched to where his father stood at the bar and held out his hand. "I want the keys to my truck now."

"How am I supposed to get home?"

"Call me or a cab when you're through doing whatever you think you're doing."

Digging into his pocket, his dad scowled. He ignored the outstretched palm and tossed them toward Zane. He managed to catch them before they fell to the floor, then he stalked toward the door.

Kim hurried after him and nearly ran into him right outside the door. She settled her hand on his arm. "Do you know who his sponsor is?"

"Yeah, Ian."

"Call him. Let him talk with your dad. Sometimes we're too close to the situation and only make matters worse."

"I will, then I'll go back to the house and wait."

"He might not be home for a long time.

Is this my fault?" she asked, still hearing the beat of the music throbbing against the walls of the bar.

Zane turned fully toward her. "No. He was drinking long before you were in our lives. He started when Mom left and hasn't stopped. Personally, I think he's afraid of what his life will be like without living in a stupor half the time."

"I'm so sorry." Her throat closed around the last syllable.

He took her face in his large hands, rubbing his thumbs over her cheeks. "I can't thank you enough for bringing me here. Go home. I'll be fine."

She hesitated.

"Please. You've got to teach a classroom of students tomorrow bright and early."

She nodded, still not trusting herself to say anything to him—not with her throat clogged with emotions she didn't want to feel. She thought she had problems with her father, but Zane's were much worse. She turned away and made it to her car, missing the feel of his palms against her cheeks.

An hour later, Zane paced a path from his couch to the kitchen and back. After having called Ian, all he could do now was wait for Ian to bring his dad home. But in what condition? That question plagued him as he made another trip to the kitchen. This time he went to the coffeepot and poured some of the strong brew into a mug. It was going to be a long night.

When he walked back into the living room, headlights spilled through the crack in the pulled drapes. He reached the front entrance as a car door slammed. Would Dad be sober or drunk? Tension twisted his gut.

He stepped outside and came to a halt when he saw Kim mount the steps to his porch. "You shouldn't have come."

"Is your dad home yet?"

"No."

"Then I should be here. You need company until he comes home."

"No, I—" The soft expression in her eyes whisked his denial away. "Come in. Shouldn't you be home? You've got work tomorrow."

"So do you, but I can afford to miss some sleep. I'll make it up tomorrow night. I went home, grabbed something to eat and—" she lifted a sack "—brought you some since I figured you didn't take the time to eat."

"You figured right, but I don't think I can eat."

"If not, then you can put it in your refrigerator and have it later."

He held the screen door open for her. "I have some coffee if you want some."

She stepped into his entry hall. "That's great. Extra strong?"

"Yup."

"Just the way I like it."

"Me, too." Zane led the way to the kitchen.

While he poured her some coffee, Kim put the food she'd brought into the refrigerator. "There's enough for you and your dad. When you're ready, just zap it in the microwave and it's good to go."

Zane refilled his cup then waved her toward the living room. "Funny how some things go. I've been back for three years, and in the past three days, I've seen more of you than in those years."

Seated on the couch, she cradled her mug between her hands and sipped. "I guess we got good at avoiding each other in Hope."

"I'm glad we aren't anymore. There were some misunderstandings that needed to be cleared up." Zane sat across from Kim, not sure what was happening between them. He didn't want to care about her.

"Besides the twenty thousand dollars you didn't take from my dad, what else?"

"What happened when you talked with my father?"

"That wasn't a misunderstanding. He made it clear how he felt about me. Still does."

"If you feel that way, why are you here?"

"Because if you can forgive my father for what he did, then I can forgive yours. I don't want to see anyone struggle with drinking and give into it again. I don't want to be the reason he gave in to alcohol after being sober for months."

"Is that what you're thinking?"

She nodded, then lowered her head.

"Three months ago, right before the hurricane, I found Dad at that same bar, staring at a glass of whiskey. Six weeks before that Ian did because I was in New Orleans and he called Ian to come get him at another bar in town. Each time he hasn't taken a drink—yet."

"So he hadn't had a drink tonight?"

"Not according to the bartender. Though after we left, he could have."

"Because he was really upset about you working at *my* house."

"Partially, but I think there's more to it than that. Ever since the hurricane, my dad has needed to test himself. Right after the hurricane, he went days with little sleep trying to help people around here get back into their homes, find their possessions, clear their debris. I hadn't seen my father like that in years—since before Mom left."

"He had a purpose."

"Yes, that's it."

"We all need a purpose." She took a sip of her coffee then placed it on a coaster on the table next to the couch. "That may be what is happening with my father, too. He used to have a job. Somewhere to go and feel he was contributing. He's only sixty. He has many good years still, but his illness has made him feel useless, especially since the hurricane."

"So what do we do about it?"

"Find things they can do that will make them feel their self-worth. As a teacher, I know how important it is for a child to have good self-esteem. When a child doesn't, it affects everything he does. That's what is happening with my dad. I've been so busy with the mess created by the hurricane that I didn't see what was going on with Dad."

Zane rose, restlessness flowing through him. He began pacing again. "That's why my father has been content these months since the hurricane until recently. Most people around here didn't have as much damage as some parts of Hope. They are back in their homes. The mess has been cleared. Repairs made. A lot because of my father. Now he doesn't have anything."

"I think your dad liked how he felt when he was helping the neighbors."

Stopping near Kim, Zane drew her to her feet. "Lately I was realizing my dad needed a job, something at least part-time, but I didn't realize why. But everything you've said fits what's happening with him. Thanks for helping me see that."

"You're welcome."

"You're a wise woman. No wonder the kids in your class love you."

She blushed and tried to cover her reaction with her hands. "Okay, I'm thoroughly embarrassed now."

"Why?"

She looked down. "I've never been comfortable with compliments."

He placed his palms over her hands, gliding them away from her face. Then he tilted her chin up so she peered into his eyes. "That hasn't changed. You weren't when we dated. Just smile and thank me."

She gave him a brilliant smile and said, "Thank you."

Entwining his fingers through hers, he hauled her toward him until his mouth hovered over hers. "See, that wasn't so hard."

"I survived," she said in a quavering rush.

"I'm glad." He leaned down, their breaths tangling.

His heartbeat kicked up a notch, and his senses became alert to everything about Kim—her jasmine scent, the softness of her hands in his work-toughened ones, her petiteness next to him. He brushed his lips across hers and tasted the coffee on them. He released her hands and began to enfold her against him.

A sound coming from the direction of the entry hall halted his actions. He straightened and swung his attention toward the noise. As the front door opened, Kim stepped away. With her cheeks as red as before, she turned her back on his father and Ian entering the living room.

"I'll take these into the kitchen." Kim gathered up the mugs and hurried away.

His father frowned. "What is she doing here?"

Ian glanced from Zane to his dad. "I'm going to see if there's any more of that coffee."

When the police chief left, Zane faced his father. "Kim is here because she was concerned about you. What's going on, Dad? How do I help you?"

The frown dissolved into a look of sorrow. "I don't know. I—I'm confused."

Zane closed the space between them. "About what?"

"I enjoyed working on the roof today. But the second I saw you and Kim together talking like fifteen years never happened, I got…" He dropped his gaze to the floor.

"Angry?"

"No, scared."

"Scared about what?"

His father looked directly at him. "These past months we have started to form a—" he fluttered his hand in the air "—a bond. I wasn't a good father to you when you were growing up. I thought finally I would get a second chance. If you two get together, where does that leave me? I don't have anything really. I've made a mess of my life."

A tightness gripped Zane's throat. "You're my dad. That will never change. You'll always be in my life."

"For twelve years you stayed away from Hope because of Kim. What if you two get together, have a fight and you leave again?"

"We're not getting together. I'm help-ing someone in need. I've been doing that in Hope. Kim is just another person who needed help. My past is just that—my past. And Kim is part of that past."

"But I've seen you with her. It's like you never left."

"No, we both are very aware that fifteen years have passed. We're becoming friends. That's all." It couldn't be anything besides that. Their relationship and what happened because of it affected so many people adversely. He wouldn't risk that again. "Are you hungry? Maggie fixed some roast chicken tonight, and Kim brought us some." He put his arm around his father and hugged him briefly.

When Zane and his dad went into the kitchen, Ian and Kim stood at the counter near the coffeepot talking. They stopped and rotated toward them.

"I was just telling Ian I needed to get home. Tomorrow is a school day. The kids will be raring to go after the long weekend." Kim put her mug into the sink and smiled at his dad. "Mr. Davidson, I'm glad you're all right. I appreciated your help today. Thanks."

Kim strolled toward the door into the dining room. His father stepped into her path. Zane tensed.

"I'm sorry for my behavior earlier," his father murmured, not quite meeting her eyes. "I shouldn't have gotten mad."

She reached out and clasped his arm, totally focused on his dad. "I understand. I hope you'll help Zane tomorrow. The storm is moving in faster than they thought. We sure could use all the help we can get. The roof needs to be finished by tomorrow night."

His dad moved out of the way. "We'll see."

"Good night, everyone." Kim continued toward the front door.

"Kim, wait up. I'm right behind you," Ian called out, took a last swallow of his coffee and set his mug in the sink. "Tom, call anytime day or night if you need to talk. I wish I could help tomorrow, but I'm on duty. I'll let myself out."

When the sound of the front door closing drifted to Zane, the silence of the house settled around him. He glanced at his dad. A thoughtful expression on his face made him pause. "Are you okay?"

"Actually, I am. I think I will help you tomorrow. It's gonna take a lot of hard work to get that whole roof shingled in one day. You certainly can't do it by yourself."

"Nope, Dad. I could use you."

"Great. I'm starved. Let's see what Kim brought us for dinner."

Zane spied the clock in the kitchen. Eleven. "A very late dinner."

"Better late than never." His dad's laughter filled the kitchen.

It was a sound that Zane hadn't thought he would hear this evening.

His dad went to the refrigerator to get the food. Tired but relieved, Zane scrubbed his hands down his face. He would eat with his father even if he wasn't hungry. Something changed tonight between them—something that Kim started.

On Tuesday after school, Kim turned into the driveway of her house to find a crew of men working diligently at shingling the roof before the rain hit. She parked and climbed from her car, staring west at the darkening sky. The storm system had picked up even more speed and probably would dump rain on them within the hour. Anna and Brady were already cleaning up the debris the workers had scattered over the ground.

Kim went inside and quickly put her purse and book bag on the counter in the game room, then returned outside to see if there was anything she could do to help. Dressed in slacks, a shirt and comfortable flat shoes, she decided not to take the time to change clothes.

Kim backed up until she could see the top of the roof. Zane must have pulled six men from another project to do this. His father came to the side where the ladder was. Kim headed toward it as the older man put his foot on the top rung.

"Can I help? Do you need something?" Kim shouted up at Mr. Davidson.

He glanced down. "We're running low on nails."

"I'll bring them up. Where are they?"

He gestured toward the back of Zane's truck. Kim scurried to it and snatched up the box, then rushed back to the ladder. Climbing halfway up, she met Mr. Davidson and handed off the nails to him, and he proceeded up to the roof. Could she do anything up there to help? She started up the rungs and went another six. Then she made the mistake of looking down at the ground. A light-headedness took hold. She squeezed her eyes closed and clutched the ladder.

"Mom, what's wrong?" Anna called from below.

"Nothing. I'll be down in a sec." But she didn't open her eyes, and she didn't move. She knew she didn't like heights, but she was only maybe twenty feet off the ground. What was wrong with her? Still, she remained frozen, glued to the ladder.

"Mom!"

Anna's shouts penetrated Kim's mind. The ladder moved. She inched her eyes open and stared down. Seeing her daughter halfway up sent panic through her. "Don't, Anna. Stay there."

"But—"

"Get down. You could fall," Kim yelled, a childhood memory swamping her with chills. She could remember climbing a ladder, a cousin shaking it and her tumbling down to the ground, followed by a visit to the emergency room. She'd suffered a broken ankle that still ached when it rained. It was aching right now.

When Anna reached the bottom, Kim inhaled a calming breath that only relieved her tension for a few seconds. She still needed to descend. She could do it. She had to. Otherwise, how would the men get down from the roof?

When a drop of rain fell on her head then another, she gripped the ladder tighter. She had to do something now. She looked up at the dark sky above her, clouds rolling across. Wind whipped her hair about her face. Some more raindrops splattered her.

Zane appeared at the top, peering down at her. "Do you need help?"

"No, no. I can get down. Are y'all finished?"

"Not quite. When it starts raining, I'll have most of my men come down. But I should be able to finish up pretty fast."

Wind, rain and an uncovered roof were not a good combination. "Everyone should come down. Including you."

"Don't worry about me. You climb down now. I'm not leaving here until I see you doing that."

Looking at the worry in his expression fortified her. She was not going to fall, especially if she could move before the rungs got too wet. "I'm going."

Her gaze fastened onto her right hand, she willed her fingers to loosen its grip one finger at a time. When her hand was free, she clenched the rung at her chest level. Then she did the same with her left hand. After slipping one foot off, she fumbled for the slat below her, not wanting to peer down. When she found it, she slid her shoe firmly into place and moved the other foot. One rung then another, she slowly made her way to the ground, feeling Zane's continual perusal. Strangely it gave her comfort instead of making her nervous.

When she planted both feet on the ground, she hugged the ladder for a moment as the rain increased to a light drizzle. Her hair still dancing about her head, she finally stepped away and stared up at Zane.

He gave her a nod and disappeared, but shortly his men began to descend the ladder, hauling tools down.

"Anna. Brady. Get inside." Kim didn't move although her clothes were becoming drenched.

A rumble of thunder sounded in the distance, but she didn't see a flash of lightning. The force of the wind increased. She bridged the distance between her and the ladder and held it steady as the first man was only a few feet above the ground.

"Mom, how about you?" Anna asked as she walked toward the back steps up to the second-story gallery.

"I'll be there in a little bit." She stepped behind the ladder to clutch both sides of it.

Finally the last worker descended, leaving Zane and his dad up on the roof. The rain came down steadily at a forty-degree angle, but she wouldn't go inside—not until Zane and his dad were safely on the ground.

Chapter Seven

"Son, we need to leave," Zane's father said over the noise of the rain hitting the roof.

"Only this one section and it will be done. Go on down. I won't be long." Zane lined up the shingle, and using the nail gun, he fastened it to the roof.

"I'm not leaving, either, then." His dad got the next shingle for Zane to nail to the roof. "It's getting slippery up here."

Still they worked. Ten minutes later as the rain slashed at them, Zane finished and quickly gathered his nail gun. "Go, Dad. It's really picking up."

His father carefully scaled his way toward the ladder. When he approached it and picked up his foot to swing down onto the first rung, his other one slipped out from under him. He fell onto the newly installed shingles and kept sliding toward the edge. He fought to get a grip, the supplies in his hand tumbling toward the ground.

Zane scrambled toward his dad, lurching to catch him before he went over the side. Grabbing hold of a vent sticking up, Zane used it as an anchor and stretched to hook his father seconds before he plunged to the ground. Zane pulled him up a few feet until his dad managed to stabilize himself. After a few breaths, he secured his foot on the top rung and stepped over the edge.

"I'm not going down until you're over here," his dad shouted over the noise of the increasing downpour.

When Zane made it to the edge, his father descended several rungs. Zane looked over and saw Kim below, drenched but holding the ladder steady for them. When his dad was far enough down, Zane swung himself over the side and followed him to the ground.

"Let's get out of the rain," Kim said and started for the steps.

His father trailed her as Zane took the ladder down, then hurried after the pair. Upstairs inside the game room, he and his dad stayed by the door while Kim dashed to the linen closet for towels.

"We should have just gone home." His father rubbed himself as dry as possible.

Zane did, too, then bent over and mopped up the puddle on the hardwood floor. "We're putting the roof on so you won't have water inside, and look how much we brought in."

"Me, too." Kim tried to dry her hair, but wet curls hung about her face. "You're both welcome to stay for dinner. I can put your clothes into the dryer."

"Thanks but I still have to go to the school tonight to make up for pulling part of the crew off the job. I'll go home and change then go there."

"I'm coming with you, son."

"Great."

"I can come, too." Slinging the towel around her shoulders, she finger-combed her hair.

"You know how to put down a gym floor?" Zane asked, remembering how she had stayed outside in the rain and held the ladder for them.

"No, but maybe I could do something else."

He grinned. "I appreciate the thought, but we'll take care of it."

"Then let me get y'all two slickers to use."

"That, I will accept." Zane took their towels and put them on the counter.

Kim came back a minute later with two yellow ones and gave each of them one. "Were you able to finish the roof?"

"Yup and this rain will be a good test to see what kind of job we did today." Zane shrugged into the slicker.

His father headed toward the door to the gallery. "I'll be out in the truck."

"Mr. Davidson," Kim called out. When his father paused and glanced back, she walked to him and continued. "Thanks for your help. If you hadn't, we'd still have part of our roof off. If I can return the favor, please let me know."

His father lowered his gaze for a few seconds then reestablished eye contact with Kim. "It was my pleasure." He opened the door, a gust of wind slamming it against the wall.

Kim grasped the door to shut it after Zane and his dad left. As she was swinging it closed, she caught Zane's gaze. At his warm look, a few stones of the wall about her heart crumbled. She owed him more than money for his repairs, and she intended to pay him.

When the lock clicked into place, Kim leaned back against the door, rubbing her hands up and down her arms. The chill of the damp wind had burrowed into her. But then she visualized Zane's last glance, and the cold melted.

Maggie entered the game room. "I can't believe we don't have to put the pans out to catch the leaking water."

"And then listen to the *drip, drip.* I can see why people think that's a torturous sound, especially when we had so many. Is Dad in his room?"

"No, I'm right here." Kim's father shuffled into the room. "I'm just glad it's quiet now."

At that moment, lightning flashed, followed almost immediately by thunder. Kim pressed her lips together to keep from laughing at the irony of it.

But it didn't stop Maggie from saying, "That's not my idea of quiet. We need to be extra thankful tonight for a dry place. I came home for lunch, and Zane and his crew didn't even want to stop to eat."

Her dad grumbled something under his breath.

Kim balled her hands into fists, her fingernails cutting into her palms. "I've had enough of your attitude. Zane didn't have to help us. He chose to because that's the kind of man he is. You staying in your room and hiding was wrong. You taught me better than that when I was growing up. What are you afraid of?"

His eyes grew round. He drew himself up taller, lifting his chin a notch. "I'm not afraid."

"You're striking out at someone who doesn't deserve it. That usually means a person is afraid of something."

"People don't change. I remember how he was fifteen years ago. His father—"

Kim held up her palm. "Stop. His father was one of the men up there fixing our roof, staying even when it started to rain so it could be finished. People do change. I have. Zane has. He isn't the same as he was when he was nineteen."

"How do you know that for sure?" He gripped the edge of the counter nearby.

"I just do."

"At church, Zane and Gideon are doing a great job with the younger kids in the eight- to twelve-year-old youth group." Maggie walked toward the door. "I'll leave you two to talk."

"Stay, Maggie. I'm leaving." Her father pivoted and headed out of the room.

When he left, Kim sank into the chair near her, her body quaking. "I shouldn't have said anything, but I'm so tired of being in the middle. Dad isn't usually this unbending."

Maggie sat across from her. "I think you're right. He's scared."

"Of what?"

"Losing you."

"To Zane? That's not going to happen. Our time has passed."

"Do you really think that?"

"I wouldn't say it if I didn't think it. After Scott, I'm in no hurry to be in another marriage. Although I do feel Zane has changed, he did leave me years ago. Anna doesn't need any more disruptions in her life."

"Just Anna?"

"Okay, me, too. We'll get this house

fixed up, and our life will settle back into its usual routine from before the hurricane."

Maggie stared at her. "You believe that?"

"What? That our lives will improve when we aren't living in a couple of rooms in this house?"

"Nope. That the house is the answer to all your problems."

"I know it's not going to be the answer to all of them, but you've got to admit it will make life a little less hectic. I feel like everything in my life is a mess like this house."

"Maybe your life feels like it's a mess because you haven't attended church much these past few years. If you don't want to go to Hope Community Church because of Zane, find another one. The Lord has a way of helping us straighten out our messes. And Anna should join the youth group."

"I'm not denying Anna. She goes with you or Polly. And I've been a few times."

It was always to the service that she knew Zane didn't attend.

"But you're denying yourself. Your faith was an important part of your life at one time."

She wanted to say it still was, but she couldn't. She would be lying. Kim rose. She didn't want to get into this conversation with Maggie after the long day at work. "I'll think about it."

"Good and we need to get Uncle Keith back to church. He needs to get out and get involved with the community again."

"I agree with that. He was very active before Mom died, before the business failed."

"Self-pity is destroying him. It's time we turn his focus onto others." Maggie made her way toward the refrigerator. "We'll work on persuading him to go Sunday."

Kim shook her head. She should have realized that when her cousin got something in her head she went after it like a pit bull. But what Maggie had said made sense. She needed to work out this mess her life had become and maybe the Lord could help her. She certainly hadn't done a good job by herself lately.

Kim stood to the side to let Cody Weston and Zane into the game room. "I'm glad you came tonight—" she glanced over her shoulder at her father nearby "—to help with Ruth's campaign for mayor." She held out her hand. "I'm Kim Walters."

Cody shook it. "Nice to meet you. I couldn't turn down Zane's invitation." The counselor surveyed the room. "You've got a nice crowd."

"Yes, let me introduce you to my father, Keith Sommerfield. Dad, this is Cody Weston with the Christian Assistance Coalition." After her father and Cody exchanged greetings, Kim asked, "How much longer are you going to be in Hope?"

"Until I'm not needed," Cody said with a smile, his eyes gleaming. "I'll be the last of the group to leave."

"Dad, can you introduce him to everyone here?"

Her father's forehead wrinkled. "Sure." The word came out slowly as he studied Kim's expression.

She hoped her intentions weren't written on her face, but she had never been a very good actress. If her dad thought this meeting with Cody was planned, he would escape to his room. He'd told her on numerous occasions he didn't want anyone messing with his head. He was perfectly fine the way he was.

"Do you think this will work?" she asked Zane after the two men moved farther into the game room.

"If anyone can help your dad without him realizing, it'll be Cody."

"I've been reading up on post-traumatic stress disorder, and I think my dad is suffering from that."

"That makes sense. He almost lost his home on top of losing his business these past few years. Hopefully Cody will be able to help with that. He served several tours of duty in the Middle East before he started working for the Christian Assistance Coalition." Zane scanned the people in the room. "Anyone else coming?"

"No, this is it. I'm glad. I don't think we could have fit anyone else in here, and this is a big room. How's the school coming along?"

"Behind schedule a little, but I'm determined it will be ready to open when I said it would. I know a lot of people are ready to move back in."

"You're looking at one here."

Zane touched her arm and pulled her away from the people around them. "When I'm through with the school project, I can spend more time on the rest of your home. Can you wait until then? Is there anything else that needs to be repaired right away?"

"No. We'll be fine until then now that the roof isn't leaking like a sieve. I can even start looking at the other rooms upstairs. As you know, we did what we could after the trees were removed, but the rooms weren't livable until now. Well, they will be when we finish some of the repairs in them. It'll be nice having my old bedroom back. Can you imagine three females sharing one small bedroom? Not a pretty sight at times."

Zane chuckled. "I think I can spare a couple of evenings to help you with those rooms. How's the wiring?"

"We have the electricity turned off in that part of the house."

"I can come tomorrow night and check it."

"You're an electrician?"

"That's what I learned first in this business before I branched out."

"Are you sure you can spare that time?"

"Yes. I don't want you doing anything until I look at it."

"Fine, on one condition."

One eyebrow rose. "You're giving conditions?"

"Yes. I want to help you with the school since you're running on a tight schedule. Think of something I can do."

"We've been through this. Most is stuff

you wouldn't know how to do." He studied her face. "You aren't going to let this go?"

"No, I believe one good deed deserves another."

His chest rose and fell with a deep sigh. "Fine. About all I can think of is painting the rooms."

"Done. You've got yourself a worker in the evenings and on the weekends when you start that."

Zane inched closer and lowered his voice. "Why are you having a hard time accepting my help without needing to do something for me?"

"I don't like being in anyone's debt."

"I'm not expecting anything from you except money for the supplies."

After Scott's treatment of her and what happened when the family business went under, she had become suspicious of something that looked too good to be true. "Why?"

"Because you're in need. Is that so hard to understand?"

What is your angle? Scott always had one. "Yes, after what happened between us."

"Fine. That last week before the grand opening on Friday I'll use you to paint. Is that what you want?"

"Yes, was that so hard?"

"Kind of."

"I'm sorry. I don't mean to be difficult."

"Everyone, can I have your attention?" Maggie called out from the other end of the long room.

Zane leaned close to her ear and said with a laugh, "Yes, you do."

The tickle of his breath sent goose bumps down her body. "Shh. We're going to get our instruction. As a teacher, I know the importance of listening to the directions."

"We need some people to assemble some material into campaign packets. Others to organize our neighborhood sweeps. And lastly, some to put yard signs together. After a few words from our next mayor, let me know where you want to work."

Maggie stepped to the side to allow Ruth Coleman to speak.

As Ruth greeted the helpers and offered her thanks, Zane whispered, "Which one are you gonna do?"

Kim slanted a glance at him, mischief dancing in his eyes. "How about you?"

"I asked first."

"Neighborhood sweeps."

"Oh, okay."

She faced him and put her hands on her waist. "Zane Davidson, where are you going to be?"

Miss Alice, an older lady who lived next door to Ruth, turned around a few feet in front of them and put her finger on her mouth. "Shh."

Zane clamped his lips together and shrugged his shoulders at Kim, then became quite intent on what Ruth was saying to her campaign workers.

"When I decided to run for mayor, I knew the only way I could do it was a grassroots campaign. I appreciate each one of you helping me to win this election.

After what Hope has gone through—still is—I want to help rebuild the town and make it even better than it was. I want people to see how wonderful it is to live in a town like Hope. We help our own. We band together and make sure no one is wanting."

Cheers erupted from the group gathered.

"Okay, y'all, we've got a lot of work to do tonight," Maggie shouted over the din as people began talking to each other.

Zane put two fingers into his mouth and blew a loud whistle. The sound rang in Kim's ears, but every person in the room rotated toward Zane. Kim flashed a nice shade of red. She was sure of it because her cheeks felt on fire.

"You've got the floor, Maggie." Zane waved his arm toward her cousin.

The crowd swung back toward Maggie. "Who's working on the packets?"

A flurry of hands shot up in the air, including her father and Cody standing next to him. Kim thought of changing to that group then decided that would put a damper on anything Cody was trying to establish with her dad.

Five minutes later, the neighborhood sweeps group with Gideon and Zane in charge decided to meet on the staircase. The committee members filed out of the game room to find a place to sit on the steps.

At the back of the group, Kim waited for Zane. "Why didn't you tell me you were in charge of this group?" she said in a low voice.

"My choice shouldn't affect your choice. Does it?"

"Well, no."

"Good because when I knew you before I never thought you were a chicken."

Kim's mouth dropped. "I'm not now."

"That's even better. When Gideon asked me to help him earlier, I immediately thought about you being an area coordinator."

"Which area?"

"Around your school. Who better to serve those neighbors."

"I like that. It'll give me a chance to visit the homes of my students. That's always good for a teacher."

"I figured that. You might be able to recruit some of the teachers at your school to go door to door, too." Zane passed her near the bottom of the stairs and took his place on the ground floor, facing the fifteen people assembled there.

As Zane started outlining what the object of the neighborhood sweeps would be, Kim tried to listen. But her mind drifted to what her father was doing. Had Cody been successful with him?

Two hours later, most of the workers had left except Ruth, Kathleen, Miss Alice, Gideon, Zane and Cody. They stayed to help put the game room back to the way it was before the onslaught of people had arrived at Bienville. Although Kim was tired, excitement grew in her. She'd never been a political person, but the prospects of affecting the mayoral race was invigorating.

"What do y'all think? Was it a successful planning meeting?" Ruth asked when the tables and chairs were returned to their right places and the paper coffee cups were tossed into the trash.

"Ruth, you'll make a good mayor. We need someone like you after the past few trying months." Kim's dad took a seat on the couch, others following suit. "Are you worried about something?"

"The opponent is spending a lot of money on flashy ads and spots on TV and radio."

"I like your grassroots campaign. You want to personally touch as many of the townspeople as you can. That's what we need right now. Our town needs hope."

Ruth gave Keith a smile, her gaze linked to his. "I appreciate your help. I could use someone who has dabbled in politics to help me. Will you?"

Surprise lit Kim's father's face; his eyebrows hiked up as far as they could go.

"I—I'll help you anyway I can." His usually strong voice came out in a raspy rush. He clenched his trembling hands in his lap. His surprise evolved into a blush that reddened his cheeks, especially the longer he stared at Ruth.

Her smile broadened. "That means a lot to me. You've been a councilman, and your expertise will be welcomed."

"That was years ago."

"It doesn't matter. I don't have an official campaign manager. Would you consider doing that?"

Her father flexed his hands then curled them again. "Me?" he choked out. "I don't know how to be one."

"Neither do any of us," Kathleen said, sweeping her arm around the room to indicate the others. "None of us have even worked on a campaign. You have. We can do the work if you can give us the guidance."

Kim moved to the side of the sofa and sat near her father. "It's only a couple of months. It'll be good for you."

Everyone offered him encouragement.

Her dad's regard swung from one person to the next. When it landed on Cody, it stayed.

"I agree with the others. It's a way to help the town if you believe Mrs. Coleman is the right candidate for the job," Cody said. "Tonight you were telling me how important this town is to you. How you're worried about it recovering. Do something about it."

The counselor threw down a challenge, and Kim barely managed to keep a grin from her expression. In a short amount of time, the man had read her father. He already knew Keith Sommerfield did not turn away from a challenge.

"I don't know…" Her father's words faded into silence as Ruth closed the distance between them and settled on the couch beside him.

She placed her hand on his arm. "Please, Keith. I don't like to lose. I know you don't, either. You're what I need."

Kim hadn't thought it possible, but his

blush deepened. He stared down at his clasped hands, his knuckles white. As he opened his mouth, Kim held her breath.

"I'll try it," he finally murmured too low for the people across the room to hear.

But Ruth did. She threw her arms around him and kissed him on the cheek. "Thank you. This means a lot to me."

After the congratulations, Miss Alice pushed herself to her feet. "I don't know about y'all, but this is way past my bedtime."

Ruth chuckled. "Mine, too. We'd better leave." After she rose, she faced Kim's father. "I'll come by tomorrow, and we'll talk more. Is ten o'clock okay?"

As though stunned by the events of the past few minutes, her dad nodded his head slowly.

After Gideon, Kathleen, Ruth and Miss Alice filed out of the game room, Maggie left to get ready for bed and to make sure Anna and Brady were settling down for the night.

Her dad stood, still looking shell-shocked. "I'd better get a good night's sleep or no telling what Ruth will talk me into tomorrow."

Cody stepped forward and shook her dad's hand. "It was a pleasure getting to know you tonight. I hope you'll come down and see the Christian Assistance Coalition. You might be interested in some of the things we're doing for Hope. I can tell you really care about the town."

"Thanks for listening to an old man talk about how Hope used to be." He continued toward the hallway.

Kim waited until she heard his bedroom door close before saying, "I don't think my dad would have agreed if you hadn't given him a challenge. Thank you, Cody."

"I hope he'll come down and see me at the office. I'd like to talk with him in private about what's going on." Cody removed a card from his wallet. "My cell number is on this. Just call me." He glanced from her to Zane. "You and I will talk more about your idea, but right now I'd better go, too."

Kim walked Cody to the door, half expecting Zane to follow. But when he didn't, she went back into the main part of the room, part of her glad he'd stayed, the other leery. Each day she was around him, her feelings toward him became more tangled and confused, and she certainly didn't need to add any more bewilderment to her life.

"What did he mean about your idea?" she asked to keep the conversation centered on a neutral topic that didn't involve feelings.

"I proposed an idea about going into areas where catastrophes have occurred and assisting the people in rebuilding their homes."

"How?"

"By starting a foundation tied with the Christian Assistance Coalition. They already help by providing food, clothing, even some temporary shelters, as well as counseling for victims. I want to take it a step further. Cody is interested and wants me to write up a proposal to present to the organization's board."

"How would it work?" The Zane she'd known as a teenager wouldn't have considered doing something like that. Or would he have? How well did she really know that Zane? There were few similarities from the boy she'd fallen in love with once and the man he'd grown up to be. At least from what she was seeing now. Could a person change that much, or had he been like that all along?

"The foundation would donate the supplies and experts to rebuild the houses and work with local contractors. They would do the work, as well as train people. It would deepen what the Christian Assistance Coalition is already doing."

"That sounds like a big undertaking."

"It will be, but there's a need in so many places in the United States and worldwide."

As Zane talked about his dream for the foundation, Kim experienced his excitement in the tone of his voice and the look on his face. Definitely this person before her was not the same boy she fell in love with years ago. The realization shook her. He had a handle on what he wanted to do whereas she was floundering, struggling to piece her life back together since Scott's betrayal, losing the family business and the hurricane.

Zane clasped her hand and drew her closer. "I'll see you tomorrow night, and we'll discuss what needs to be done upstairs."

"Come to dinner. I know you'll be working late at the school, but we can hold dinner until you can get here." The desire to melt against him blanketed her in needs she thought she would never experience again. She forced herself to keep several inches between them but not far enough apart, however, because her heartbeat raced and her breath shortened.

"Call me when you get home from school. By then I should know if I can and what time."

"Great. Maggie's cooking, so you'll be in for a treat."

He breached the space between them and wound his arms around her. "You aren't as bad as you think. I loved your spaghetti. Better than anything I'd throw together. Just ask my dad."

"How's he doing?"

"Okay. Ian came over last night and had a long talk with him. Dad was pretty upbeat after Ian left."

"Good," Kim said, trying to stifle a yawn that had welled up in her. She didn't succeed.

"I'd better leave before you fall asleep on me."

"It's been a long day." Her lips tingled with the knowledge of how close he was to her. A dip of his head and their mouths could meet in a kiss. She wanted him to kiss her.

And when he bent forward slightly, he gave her a quick one on the tip of her nose. "See you tomorrow." He released his hold on her and strode toward the door out onto the upstairs gallery.

Disappointment unfolded in Kim and spread through her. Friends. That was all they were and she needed to remember that. She had to put a halt on her developing feelings for Zane. He'd left her and the town once, and if his plans for the foundation worked out as he hoped, he would leave again.

Chapter Eight

"How did the campaign planning go tonight?" his father asked when Zane came into the house twenty minutes later that evening.

"You should have come." Zane checked the mail on the counter—mostly junk, which he tossed into the trash and kept the one bill.

"No, I don't see me doing something like that. I would like to see Ruth as our mayor, though."

"Great. She'd love your vote. I've been thinking about something."

His dad muted the TV show he was

watching and focused on Zane. "So have I. I appreciate you giving me a job, but I don't want you to feel obligated to hire your own father. If I don't carry my own weight, I need you to tell me. I don't want to be a charity case."

Zane dropped into the lounge chair across from the couch, tired from the fast pace of his day. "You aren't. I need your help. In fact, I want to see if you'll work for Kim repairing their upstairs while I get the school finished. Then I'll be able to put a couple of other men on it, too." His dad's expression remained neutral so he hurriedly added, "It would only be about two weeks. I'll even come over in the evening and do some myself. I'm going to check tomorrow night. She said something about a wiring problem."

"I'm not an electrician. I can do plumbing and general construction."

"I know. I'll work on the wiring if you can do the rest until I have more men."

"Why does it have to be finished so quickly?"

"Because her father is having trouble dealing with the destruction to his family home. Every time I see him I sense that. I can see it in his face, like he's lost. If I can restore his home, he may start to recover."

"Son, you don't owe that man anything."

"But I do owe Kim. I left her. Not the other way around."

"She found someone else."

"But they're divorced. Something went wrong because I know Kim's feelings about marriage. She only wanted to get married one time. No divorce." What had happened with her and Scott? The man had fit every criteria her family would have thought important.

"Sometimes what seems good on the surface isn't."

Zane stared at the deep lines on his father's face, put there by many years of drinking himself into forgetfulness. There had been a time when he'd first left Hope that he'd turned to alcohol until one day he woke up and didn't know how he'd ended up passed out on a bench in Jackson Square. He'd glanced at another man in the same condition, trying to figure out where he was. He'd remembered seeing his father like that many times. That was when he started to turn his life around. He would not become his father and let what happened to him in the past rule his life to the point of self-destruction.

"Are you talking about Mom? Why did she leave us?"

"Because I wasn't enough for her. She wanted something...different. I can't really blame her. If I saw her now, I would apologize to her for what happened to our marriage."

"But she left me, too." For years, Zane had kept that bottled up inside of him and hadn't said anything to his dad about her walking out.

His father studied a spot on the floor between them. "We had a big fight. I told her if she couldn't accept me for who I was then to leave. And not come back. That you and I could get along just fine without her." He raised his head and looked Zane in the eye. "She did. For a while she called to check up on you, but I wouldn't tell her anything. I told her if she wanted to know she would have to come home. It was all my fault."

Zane's throat swelled with suppressed rage. "She could have come back to see me. She decided not to." And in that moment, he realized he hadn't forgiven his mother. After all he'd said to Kim about forgiving her and her father, he harbored anger toward his mother. No wonder he didn't want to get married.

"Relationships can be complicated. I've not been very good at them. Look at ours."

"That's changing, Dad."

"Only because I'm not drinking. What if I do? I've come close several times these past six months."

"I'm here for you. You aren't alone."

His dad grinned. "That's what our police chief says to me."

"Will you help me with restoring Bienville?" Then maybe he would be totally free of the past. He had wronged Kim and wanted to right that.

"Yeah, son. It's a beautiful old home. It'll be a challenge to put it back to its former glory, but I think that's a challenge I can help with."

Zane stood. "Thanks. After I meet with Kim tomorrow night, you can get started. Good night."

Zane strolled toward his bedroom, weariness sagging his shoulders. There weren't enough hours in the day to do all he wanted to do.

"How did it go with Cody this afternoon?" Kim asked her father on the way home from seeing the counselor on Saturday.

"I know what you're doing."

She stopped at a light and slanted a glance toward him. "What?"

"You had Zane bring Cody on Wednesday so he could talk to me. You figured if I got to know him that I might talk to him about what's wrong with me. Nothing is wrong with me except I have Parkinson's disease."

"What did Cody tell you?"

"We just talked about what was going on with the house. Not much else. Oh, yes, he showed me some relaxation treatments. Because I'm having sleeping problems, he wanted me to contact my doctor. I'm perfectly fine, though."

"Getting only a few hours of sleep at night, not leaving the house much or even your room and often just lying in your bed staring at the ceiling are not normal. You've had to deal with a lot of stress over the past years with Mom's death, losing the business and being diagnosed with Parkinson's." Kim caught sight of her purse with the envelope sticking out of it. "He wants you to sign a release so he can talk to your doctor about some medication to help you."

"I take enough pills. I don't want any more."

Frustrated with his stubbornness, Kim tightened her grip on the steering wheel.

"If you knew what I was doing, then why did you go today?"

"I may have an illness, but I'm not losing my mind. I knew if I didn't go today, you would nag me until I agreed to go. I went as you wanted. Now drop it."

Kim pulled into the long driveway leading to their home. "I never said you were losing your mind, and I know Cody didn't, either. You're stressed, and it's taking a toll on you physically. You need help. I can't say it any plainer than that."

When she stopped in front of the house, her dad hurriedly opened the door and climbed out, saying, "I am not a kid. I'm your father. I will run my own life. I leave this place when I need to. I did today." Then he slammed the door and strode toward the house.

The sound reverberated through the car. Kim closed her eyes and tried to relax. She couldn't. Tension cloaked her as if it were a second skin. Tension that was so much a part of her life lately.

She reached for her purse, her fingers

brushing across the envelope with the release in it. The only other thing she could do was talk to her father's physician and let him know what was going on. Dr. Blackman might have a way of persuading her dad to at least come in and see him, if not a counselor.

With her body feeling weighed down, she pried herself from the seat and headed for the house. When she entered and started for the staircase, loud voices penetrated her weariness and sent her hurrying up the steps to the second floor. She heard her father yelling in her old bedroom, the one Mr. Davidson was working on right now.

When she rushed into the room, she found her father in Mr. Davidson's face, screaming for him to quit making so much noise and to get out of his house. Her dad trembled from head to toe and his face turned blood-red. Mr. Davidson sent a silent plea to her as she approached them.

She wedged herself between the pair,

Mr. Davidson quickly backing away as far as he could go. "Dad!"

Fury glazed his eyes. Her father's mouth opened and closed, but no words came out.

She clasped his arms to try and steady him. "Calm down. Take deep breaths."

"Stop babying me." He yanked away and stumbled back.

Kim grabbed for him to stop him from going down, but she couldn't catch him in time. He collapsed to the floor, curling himself up into a ball.

Rocking back and forth, he murmured, "I can't take the noise. First the roof and now this."

Kim swept toward Mr. Davidson and whispered, "You can use our phone in the game room. Call Zane. Let him know what has happened. Then if you can find Maggie, have her come in here. I think she's in the garden out back."

He nodded and quietly left, pausing in the doorway and throwing a look over his shoulder. Concern etched deeper lines into Zane's dad's face, reflecting how she felt.

She placed her arm around her father. "The noise has stopped. Listen. It's quiet now." She schooled her voice into a soothing tone she prayed reached him.

"What's wrong with me? I'm not crazy. I'm not crazy."

Maggie flew into the room, panting when she came to a halt next to Kim. "What do you need me to do?"

She rose and leaned toward Maggie to whisper in her ear, "Call Dr. Blackman and Cody. See if they can come here."

"Okay."

When Maggie left, Kim knelt again by her father. "I'll help you up, and we can go to your room. All right?"

He nodded, tears running down his still-red cheeks.

Grasping him against her, she slowly made her way to his bedroom. His shaking trembled through her. When she entered, she headed straight for the bed and helped her dad sit down, then took the place next to him, her arm still about him while she held one of his hands.

"I'm not crazy. I just don't…" His words ended on a sob, and he lowered his head until his chin touched his chest.

"I'm here to help, Dad. Let me. You need to let Dr. Blackman know what's going on with you. Cody needs to talk to him. There's nothing wrong with getting the help you need." She'd discovered that when she'd ignored fifteen years of heartache to ask Zane to repair Bienville.

He buried his face in his shaky hands. "I feel like I'm falling apart."

Maggie stepped into the entrance of the room and nodded her head, mouthing, "They're coming."

"Both Dr. Blackman and Cody are coming to help. Please let them." Kim stroked his back, trying to convey a calm she didn't feel inside. Seeing her father like this unnerved her more than when Scott walked away from their marriage. She'd known that was over when he'd refused to have anything to do with Anna. But she couldn't give up on her dad.

"Where's that release? I'll sign it. Anything to stop this." He directed his look at her. "I almost hit Tom Davidson. I just lost it."

"Maggie, I left my purse with the release in my bedroom. Will you get it for me?"

Her cousin left, returning a minute later with Kim's purse. Maggie gave it to her.

After digging in her bag for a pen, Kim unfolded the release and placed it on the hard surface of her purse for him to sign. Her dad scribbled his signature, then sank back on his bed. Closing his eyes, he laid his arm across his forehead and drew air in through his nose then released it through his pursed lips.

A bell chimed, indicating someone was at the upstairs back door in the game room. Maggie whirled around and went to answer the door. Kim rose and lifted her father's legs onto the bed.

"Are you feeling better?" she asked him.

He inhaled and exhaled several more

deep, relaxing breaths. "I don't lose control."

Kim glanced at the doorway. "Dr. Blackman is here to see you."

The man entered, and Kim met him halfway across the room. She moved close to tell the doctor what happened with Mr. Davidson.

She was halfway through the description of what she saw when her father pushed himself up on his elbows and said, "You don't have to whisper. It's no secret that I screamed like a banshee at Tom for using his electric saw to fix my house—something that needs to be repaired and I want repaired. Charles, I lost it."

"Let me check you out, then we'll talk. It may be a good thing for you to go to the hospital."

"No. No hospitals. My wife went to one and never returned home."

"I'll be in the game room, Dr. Blackman. Dad's new counselor is coming. He and Dad talked today. He might have some insight."

"Dr. Weston arrived when I did. I've worked with him concerning several of my patients." The doctor walked to the bed and put his black bag on the table next to it.

Kim closed the door and went to the game room where Mr. Davidson, Zane, Maggie and Cody waited for her. Kim's gaze shifted from one to the other, detecting worry in their expressions.

She bridged the distance to Tom Davidson. "I'm sorry for what happened in the bedroom. My father isn't himself."

"I know. I understand."

For a long moment, the connection between her and Mr. Davidson remained as though no one else was in the room. Everything in the past didn't matter anymore to Kim. She saw genuine sympathy in the older man's eyes. Had some of what her father was experiencing been like what he'd gone through with his addiction to alcohol? The loss of control. The denial. The anger festering inside.

Zane appeared at her side. "How about you? Are you okay?"

"Honestly? I don't know what I'm feeling right now. On the ride back from Cody's office, we talked about what was going on, and he denied he had a problem." Kim peered toward the counselor. "He refused to sign the release. At least in the car." She held out the paper. "He did after he lost it. I hate that it took those actions to get him to acknowledge something is wrong, but maybe something good will come out of it."

"I don't know about y'all, but I could use a big cup of coffee." Maggie strolled to the kitchen part of the room and began making a pot.

Kim sank onto the couch, wishing the soft cushions could swallow her up, shield her from what was going on. She was glad the kids were at friends' houses today. The words spewing from her father's mouth had burned her ears. She'd never imagined hearing him talk like that. He'd always been an example of a Southern gentleman, but the man in that room a while ago hadn't been the father she knew.

While Kim rested her head on the back of the sofa, Zane, Cody and Mr. Davidson took a seat.

"Kim, what do you want us to do about making repairs?" Zane settled next to her on the couch.

"I don't know. Dad wants the house back to the way it was. I think that will help him."

"It'll be hard to do without making noise." Mr. Davidson crossed his legs and took the mug of coffee Maggie passed to him.

"I know. What do you think, Cody?" Kim straightened and picked up her drink that Maggie placed on the table next to her.

"Dr. Blackman may prescribe some medication for Keith, but that may take a while to get into his system. You might have to get creative or postpone having your house repaired, which I don't think is a solution."

"Part of the problem is that Dad has been cooped up in this house way too long. I need to get him out more."

Maggie stood behind Mr. Davidson and sipped her coffee. "Why not see if Ruth can help us? Uncle Keith has agreed to be her campaign manager. Maybe she can get him out of the house to work on her campaign."

"I imagine you wouldn't have to do it for long. He's hypersensitive about things like sound and touch right now, but with the right medication, he'll be able to cope." Cody glanced toward the doorway.

Dr. Blackman came into the room. "I could use a cup of that great-smelling coffee."

While Maggie went to fill him a mug, he sat in the last vacant chair and put his bag on the floor next to him.

"How's Dad?"

"I've given him something to help him sleep. He's exhausted. Why didn't he tell me he wasn't sleeping when I saw him a few weeks ago?"

"You know Dad. He hates to admit to anything being wrong. The insomnia has gotten worse in the past week or so." It was about the time Zane had come back into their lives. Had she added to her father's stress? All she'd wanted to do was make their situation better so her dad would become himself again. She peered toward Zane and became trapped in his dark blue eyes. She saw the same question in his gaze.

"Dr. Weston, I understand Keith signed a release for us to talk. Do you have a few minutes right now?"

"Yes."

Kim rose. "We'll leave you two alone, then."

Zane came to his feet at the same time his father did. "I need to get back to the school. Dad, why don't you come help me there?"

"Sure, son."

Maggie left the house first and headed toward her garden. While Mr. Davidson descended the staircase, Zane remained on the landing.

He grasped Kim's hand. "Dad really is okay about what happened."

"I'm not. My dad scared me. I've never seen him like that. He doesn't lose it."

"We all have the capability to lose it at any time."

"Yeah, that's called stress, and it's taking its toll on Dad."

Pulling her to him, he held both of her hands, the only barrier between them. "How about you? What's happening has to be affecting you, too."

Her pulse rate accelerated. She wouldn't be surprised if he felt it beneath his fingertips near her wrist. "I'm not quite ready to go running down the street stark raving mad. A few more months like the last ones, however, might change that."

The corners of his mouth hitched up. "Just give me fair warning so I can run for cover."

"Chicken."

"You got it. A smart man learns from

his mistakes. A really smart man learns from other people's mistakes."

The warmth in his eyes and touch urged her to snuggle against him. She tamped down that feeling. She didn't need to add more stress to her already-strained life, and getting involved with Zane again would do just that. He wasn't the answer for her—only a diversion she couldn't afford. Right now her father needed her, and that was where she should put all her energy.

He grazed his finger across her cheek. The roughened pad illustrated a man who worked with his hands. "Take care of yourself or you won't be able to take care of your father." After giving her a quick hug, he stepped back, dropping his arms to his sides. "When you figure out what you want me and Dad to do about the house, let me know."

"I will." She leaned back against the wooden railing of the gallery and watched him take the stairs down to the ground.

At the bottom, he peered back at her

and smiled—that brilliant, dazzling one that rivaled the sun on a bright day. She nearly melted into the floor of the gallery. Strengthening her grip on the wood, she managed to stay upright.

After Zane disappeared from view, she stared at the door into the game room. She should go in and see what Dr. Blackman thought after talking with Cody. But she couldn't just yet. She rounded the side of the house and walked to the front. From this height she could glimpse the Gulf in the distance. The water reminded her of Zane's eyes—blue and glittering in the sunlight.

She needed to spend less time with Zane and more time with her dad. He needed to be reassured their life would return to normal in due course—even if she had to wait to get the interior of the house back to the way it was. She would do what she could to the upstairs until her father was better. His well-being was top priority.

For a few moments longer, she relished the light cool breeze laced with a salty tang before she went back into the game room. Both men looked toward her when she came inside.

Taking a chair, she folded her hands in her lap and asked, "Have y'all decided what's wrong?"

"Dr. Weston feels that your dad is suffering from post-traumatic stress disorder. I've seen some cases since the hurricane and so has Dr. Weston. But I'll know more after I run some tests. I want your father in my office first thing on Monday. Once I rule out something going on with his illness, I'm encouraging your dad to talk with Dr. Weston on a regular basis for a while. I'll prescribe some medication that should help his anxiety and depression while he's getting counseling to deal with the stress. He has a lot of anger built up that he needs to find a better outlet for."

"What about continuing the repairs on the house?" Her role had shifted over the past few years as her dad's illness had progressed, which probably fueled his stress and anger, too. He had been the provider for the family. Now he had to depend on her.

Dr. Blackman and Cody exchanged looks before the counselor said, "We discussed this. I think ultimately the repairs to the house are important to your father's frame of mind. Give me a couple of weeks to work with him and for the medication to take effect. Then you should be able to resume work, especially if you're able to get him out of the house more. I'm not sure even I could take constant hammering and sawing without breaks."

"Now that our roof has been replaced, that should work out for everyone." And the time away from Zane would give her a reprieve, a chance to deal with her changing feelings for him.

Chapter Nine

Over a week later, Zane approached Kim in the hall at Hope Community Church after the late service. "I was beginning to think you were avoiding me again."

"Again? Me?" Mischief flirted with her blue gaze.

"Yes, and you know exactly what I'm talking about, but then I did my fair share of avoiding you, too."

She tilted her head to the side and peered up at him through lowered eyelashes, something she often did when she was trying to make a point. "Except for the house, when do we see each other?"

"What prompted you to come to the late service? Usually when you come to church it's the early one." Before, he'd known that was her routine when she did come to church and made sure to avoid the early service as she had the late one.

"Dad. He wanted to come this Sunday, and first service is too early for him. He doesn't move as fast as he used to, so it takes him longer to get going in the morning."

The Keith Sommerfield he'd known years ago had been a power to reckon with. There was little left of that person, stamped out by the disasters that had befallen him. When Zane was younger he would have gloated over that. Not now. He'd wanted revenge, but he'd never wished for the man to lose his business and a good part of the land surrounding his family home. Those losses had stripped the man of his identity.

Zane searched the large room and found Keith talking to his father. "Your dad is looking better. Should we rescue them?"

He nodded toward the pair on the other side of the hall.

"No, one of the reasons he came this morning was Maggie said your father has been coming lately with you. Dad needed to apologize again to him. He's been talking with Cody every other day for the past week and working through some of his problems. That man is perfect to work with my father. He won't let him get away with much."

"If there are no more supply problems, the school will be finished after this week. You asked me to schedule your home repairs after that."

"So the school might not be ready to move into this coming weekend?"

"It's gonna go down to the wire to be ready by Friday for the decorating committee to prepare for the grand opening."

"What supply problems?"

"Things like the paint. There was a fire at the factory that has shut down their operations for a few days. I'm thinking of painting the rooms orange or cherry red."

"Oh, please, no. That's bound to cause the children to bounce off the walls. Cool green or blue would be better."

"It might be that or plasterboard white."

"White I can live with." She hesitated for a moment then said, "Remember, I offered to help paint if you needed an extra pair of hands. Maggie, too."

"I can't ask you—"

"Zane, I've got a proposition for you. We'll paint, and you can deduct what you think we're worth from your bill for repairing our house. I know you aren't charging us for labor so consider it your tip."

Laughter welled up in him. "Tip? You make me sound like a waiter."

"There's nothing wrong with waiting tables. Didn't you do that for a while in high school?"

"Yes, my second job to earn money for—" He suddenly snapped his mouth closed.

"For what?"

He stared at their fathers still having a

conversation. His dad had a neutral expression on his face. Not bad, considering how he'd felt about Keith Sommerfield several weeks ago.

"Zane?"

"For prom and—" he cleared his throat as thoughts of that night fifteen years ago flitted through his mind "—for your engagement ring."

"My engagement ring? You never said anything about that."

"It was gonna be a surprise the night of prom." It hadn't been much—a fourth of a carat diamond—but to him it had been simple and elegant, something that personified Kim. Sitting in jail that evening, he'd realized he'd been a fool to think it was enough for Kim. She'd deserved so much better, and he couldn't give it to her. At nineteen, he'd thought material objects were important. Now he knew there was a lot more than that. Material possessions didn't keep the loneliness at bay.

"Oh. A lot changed that night."

"I grew up fast."

"So did I."

His gaze bound to hers, the air charged between them. "I'll give you a call about the painting. It may not be until Wednesday or Thursday."

"Cutting it close."

"Yup. But it should dry overnight in time for the decorating committee."

"Are you going to the grand opening?"

"I love a good Mardi Gras party."

"Costume and all?"

"I've been known to don one in New Orleans."

"This I've got to see."

Her scent of jasmine toyed with his senses. Her nearness even in a sea of people affected his heart rate. He probably shouldn't ask this, but he'd missed her this past week. He'd even driven by her house late one night—not a good sign.

"Do you want to go together?" The invitation came out before he could stop it.

"A date?"

Although he hadn't had time to go on many dates lately, working sixteen-hour days, he'd done his share of dating. But at the moment the word terrified him, its implication taking what was happening between them to a whole new level. "That's up to you." He was a chicken, avoiding a direct answer, but her expression had settled into a neutral one, much like his father's a few minutes ago—one he couldn't read, one that gave him no indication of where he stood with her.

"Then let's keep it between friends."

"Of course," he murmured, trying to keep the disappointment from his voice. "I can pick you up at seven on Friday. What about Anna?"

"She can go with Maggie and Brady."

"That's okay. Have her come with us."

Her attention fixed on a spot behind Zane. A smile spread across her mouth. "Are you ready to leave, Dad?"

Zane stepped to the side as Keith joined them. "It's nice to see you at church, sir."

"It's been a while." Kim's father swiveled toward her. "Ruth and I are going out to eat at the café to talk campaign strategies."

"Good. I'll see you later at home then for dinner."

"Maybe. Her opponent is running a negative campaign. We need to work out how to address his innuendoes."

"I hadn't heard."

Her father frowned. "Just started yesterday in an interview he gave Mrs. Calvin for her blog. She posted it last night. Not flattering at all. I'll see you when I see you." Keith weaved his way through the crowd to Ruth. Putting his hand at the small of her back, he escorted her from the hall.

"Gideon said your dad went over to Ruth's a couple of afternoons this week."

"Yeah, I didn't even have to orchestrate that. He took it upon himself." Kim's attention turned to Zane. "I never thought I would hear the word *blog* in my dad's vocabulary. When it comes to technology, he's gone kicking and screaming into the twenty-first century."

"I've heard about Mrs. Calvin's blog. She talks about the stuff that happens around the town. Dad has told me she has a humorous outlook on life."

"I'll have to check it out. I haven't known Mrs. Calvin to take sides in something like this."

"If it was an interview, then it wasn't necessarily her opinion. But my curiosity has been piqued." He caught sight of Anna waving toward Kim. "Is she staying for the youth group?"

"Yes, and Brady, too."

"Good. I see Gideon leaving. We're going to the park with the kids to play basketball. I think he's determined to teach me or humiliate me in the process."

"I'll warn you. Anna is good. Get on her team."

"Will do."

As he strode toward the double doors into the hall, he tried to stamp out his disappointment they weren't going to the Mardi Gras party as a couple. But it was her choice and probably for the best.

* * *

In the full-length mirror on her closet door, Kim surveyed herself in the yellow taffeta hoop gown, her hair done up in a coiffure of curls that cascaded down her back. It was a far cry from how she'd looked when she'd returned home late last night after painting at the school for hours. She'd always thought of herself as neat and meticulous, but one look at herself in this very mirror last night—with paint everywhere—she'd had to revamp that assessment. But Zane had needed all the assistance he could get in order for the Mardi Gras party to take place this evening.

"You've still got some paint on the back of your arm." Maggie pointed at Kim's left one.

Kim rotated until she could see it in the mirror. Laughter sprinkled the air. "Good catch. If I'm going to dress up as a Southern belle, then I need to look the part. Paint on my arm sorta kills the vision of a life of leisure." Kim traipsed to the bathroom to wet a washcloth and scrubbed off the pale blue paint before returning to the bedroom. "Is it all gone?"

"Yes. Now you have a red blotch where you rubbed it off."

"That's going to be the least of my worries. How are we going to sit in these hoop skirts? For that matter, walk through a doorway?"

"Delicately."

"Or we'll be the sensations of the party."

"I heard the upstairs doorbell. That must be Zane. Where's Anna?"

"Letting Zane inside right about now. She wanted to show him her milkmaid costume."

Maggie headed for the hallway. "I'm rounding up Brady and Uncle Keith. After we pick up Ruth, we'll be at the school."

Having to go sideways through the doorway, Kim made her way to the game room where she found her daughter sitting on a stool pretending to milk a cow. Her giggles echoed through the air. But it was Zane who demanded Kim's attention.

Dressed as a pirate with a black patch over one eye, he looked like a handsome rogue, who was not her date, she reminded herself. They were going as friends. But for days that thought had left her disappointed, wanting more.

"Where did you learn how to milk a cow?" he asked Anna though his gaze brushed down Kim's length in a leisurely survey before returning to her face.

"Papa Keith. He did it when he was a little boy back a looong time ago. I'm glad I don't hafta milk a cow to get my milk for my cereal every morning. I might never get to school." Anna saw Kim and hopped to her feet, her white mob cap sitting lopsided on her head.

Glancing away from Zane, Kim approached her daughter and straightened the cap. "Now you look like a proper maid."

"Maid? Just so you know, I don't do windows." Anna covered her mouth and more giggles spilled out between her fingers.

"Silly. You know it means a young woman." Kim felt the scorch of Zane's eyes and shifted from side to side, resting her hands on her full skirt of yellow taffeta as it rocked with her movements.

"Y'all both look wonderful as young maids." Zane's husky Southern drawl nipped at the tight control she had on her emotions. Friends only, she reminded herself.

Kim finally locked gazes with Zane. Her throat grew dry, and her pulse began to pound against her veins, throb in her head. "You look interesting. Where's the parrot that should be on your shoulder?"

"I knew I left something at home. I guess it's just me tonight."

The intensity in his regard robbed her of a coherent reply. She observed his mouth moving as he said something to her daughter, but the words didn't register in her brain. This man before her, within arm's reach, was anything but a pirate. He was caring and giving to others. There had been hints of that when they had dated as teenagers, but she liked very much what she saw now—a compassionate person who gave away a lot of the money he made.

She became aware of her surroundings slowly as she realized Anna was waving her hand in front of Kim's face. "I want to go. I'm meeting my friends, Mom."

Kim blinked, inhaled a deep breath and smiled, the corners of her mouth quivering. "Don't you know a lady is supposed to keep people waiting?"

Anna pointed at herself. "Not this lady. Let's go." She charged for the door, flung it open and headed down the stairs, the sound of her footfalls loud.

"I guess she wants to go," Kim said with a chuckle and trailed after her daughter.

Behind her, Zane said, "You probably should ride in back by yourself. I'm not sure your gown will fit in the front with me."

Tossing a glance over her shoulder, she hiked her dress up a little as she carefully maneuvered the steps sideways. "That's

fine by me. I always wanted to be chauf-
feured."

On the ground level, he swept his arm
across his body. "At your service." Then
he moved to the back door of his truck and
opened it. "Not exactly a limousine but it
will have to do."

As Kim settled onto her seat, fighting
to keep the material of her dress down,
Anna's giggles erupted yet again. "We
traded places, Mom. Like that movie I
love to watch."

Kim gave her hoop skirt a shove down
and laid her arms across it. "When we
get to the party, I want you to stay in the
gym unless you let me know where you're
going."

Zane slipped in behind the steering
wheel, flipped up his black patch so he
could see and winked at Anna. "Aye,
matey. Ready to take this wench to our
ship?"

"Ship? You're silly."

"Hey, I have a sailboat. We could skip
this shindig and go sailing."

"At night?" Anna grinned from ear to ear.

The whole way to the school Zane and Anna continued to carry on as if Kim wasn't even there, discussing where they would go if they sailed away. Listening to their conversation made her wonder if Zane had ever wanted to be a father. When they had been young, they had talked about starting a family in the future—the distant future. Why hadn't Zane ever married? Had those children?

At the school, her daughter spied Polly with Lily, Anna's cousin on Scott's side of the family. "Polly's been hanging with Lily more and more. I gotta go."

"Be nice, Anna."

"Well, Lily needs to be." Anna jumped from the cab and ran to catch up with her friend, leaving Kim to try and make a graceful exit from the truck.

Zane opened her door and offered her a hand. She fit hers in his and with the other held down her gown as she turned to the side and stepped down onto the running board.

"If I wore glass slippers, I would feel like I'm Cinderella—" she paused for several heartbeats "—meeting the pirate of the Caribbean."

"I guess we should have coordinated our costumes," Zane commented to her when they entered the gym and noticed half the couples were dressed in outfits that complemented each other.

"I like Gideon's dragon costume that goes with Kathleen's fair damsel in distress."

Zane bent close. "Look. The mayor and his wife are Hansel and Gretel."

"Oh, there are my neighbors dressed as Romeo and Juliet. That's romantic."

"She must have picked that costume out."

Kim chuckled. "You don't think Bob is romantic?"

"Not the Bob I went to school with. Not one ounce."

"You're right. She must have."

"Would y'all move out of the way? I'm here to look for my Rhett Butler and need to make a grand entrance." Going straight forward, Maggie wrestled with her sweeping hoop gown and popped through the doorway. "I'm gonna end up embarrassed tonight. This is the last time I let you talk me into wearing something so ridiculous. How our ancestors put up with this is beyond me."

Kim barely got out of the way before Maggie plowed into the gym because right behind her came Kim's father escorting Ruth costumed as the Mad Hatter and the Queen of Hearts. "I knew Dad was going to pick up Ruth, but I didn't know they planned to come as a couple."

"Gideon told me your dad is really taking the job as campaign manager seriously. Remember those neighborhood sweeps? He's scheduled them for Saturday in two weeks. They want teams of two to cover different streets. Ready to go house to house?"

"The area around the school is one of the most damaged in Hope. This will give me a chance to see my students in their homes without them thinking I'm checking up on them. There are a few I'm concerned about."

"Who? Maybe there's something I can do to help them."

"There's one family especially. The father is proud. Barely made ends meet before the hurricane and wouldn't accept any charity. After Naomi, they lost their home. The foundation was all that was left. They lived in a shelter until they could move back to their property. They have a trailer in the driveway. That must be where they live now. I don't know that they will be able to rebuild."

"Where?"

She gave him the address on Decatur Street.

"With the school finished, I have a little breathing room. That'll free up my largest team. A few of them I'm putting on your house. Do you still want us to start next week?"

"Yes. Dad is gone more and more lately."

"Great, because my father can't wait to get back to your house. He said the place has character, and he wants to bring it out." Zane offered Kim his arm. "Ready to go have fun?"

"Absolutely." As they moved farther into the gym, Kim glimpsed a big banner strung across the stage at one end of the gym/auditorium. "Look. There's a picture of you and me up there."

Zane slowed his step and averted his gaze. "Uh, I forgot to tell you they picked me to be king of the Mardi Gras party and asked me to pick my queen. Your name came to mind."

"And you're just now getting around to telling me?"

"Yeah, I told you I forgot."

"How can you forget something like that? They must have photoshopped a crown on my head."

"Mine, too. I don't go around wearing one."

"This is going to be a long evening, Zane Davidson."

* * *

Two hours later, Kim stood up on the stage next to Zane, her cheeks burning with embarrassment as the principal set a paper crown on her head. A cheer went up as the man declared Zane and her the king and queen of the Mardi Gras party. A few wolf whistles sounded above the clapping. Her blush deepened.

Gideon cupped his mouth and shouted from the front row. "Kiss. Kiss."

The rest of the audience took up the chant. She hadn't thought it possible to be any more humiliated than she already was. She found out she could be.

Zane looked at her and shrugged. He slid closer to her and turned toward her. The audience roared. After cradling her head between his hands, he slipped his fingers into her curls, nudging her nearer. A hush fell over the crowd. Inch by agonizingly slow inch, he leaned down, his lips slightly parted. A hint of peppermint laced his breath.

Anticipation tingled through her. She

didn't care that hundreds of people were watching. She wanted the kiss, and yet a small part of her feared its effect on her. His mouth whispered against hers. She melted into him.

His hands glided down her back as his lips settled over hers, coaxing them apart. They melded together as one, bodies pressed against each other. Somewhere in the distance clapping began again and rose to a crescendo. Suddenly she was thrust back into the present—one where she stood in front of a crowd on the school stage.

Zane pulled back slightly and gave her a goofy grin. "First time I've kissed someone in front of an audience."

"Me, too." She scanned the sea of people and honed in on her dad at the back, turned away talking to Ruth. His body stance relaxed, he gestured with his hands, deep into the conversation.

"I think it's time to make our exit." With his hand at the small of her back, Zane guided her offstage and excused himself.

As he started to leave, Kim caught his arm and halted his escape. "You have some explaining to do about all of this."

His grin grew as a mob of female students surrounded Kim. When Anna and Polly fought their way to the front of the group, Kim's hand slipped to her side, and Zane hurried away. Some of the girls in her class bombarded her with questions about who the man was.

"He's Mr. Davidson," Anna answered for her before Kim could open her mouth. "He's fixing our home. I get to help him."

"Yeah, and he's our youth-group leader," Polly added.

Several of the kids nodded.

Over the heads of the children, Kim spied Zane taking off his paper crown, then his shoes before stepping up to be in the charity dunking tank. She cackled as she plotted her revenge.

Zane wondered what in the world had made him agree to take his turn being in the dunking tank. The money raised would go to the school, but he'd already done his share of helping the school. Still, he had to open his big mouth and say yes to his secretary, who coordinated the different booths. Now he saw Kim shaking herself loose from the mob of girls and stalking toward him with mischievous intent in her eyes.

Then Zane glimpsed Kathleen's son Jared, who had declared at the last youth-group meeting that he was going to be the first one to cream Zane. Across the room, the boy zeroed in on him, too. But Kim managed to scoot into line in front of Jared by using her hoop skirt to block him.

Zane's gut tightened. He was gonna get wet, and if Kim had a say, it was going to be by her. She took the tennis ball and tossed it in the air, a playful smile on her face. She'd probably come back more than once. But he deserved it. He should have warned her of their royal titles before she'd come to the party.

She threw the ball straight up in the air

again and snatched it to her when it came down. "I used to play on a girls' softball team," she called out to Zane. "Did I ever tell you that?"

"No. But that was years ago. If you don't use a skill, you lose it." He knew better than to taunt her, but he might as well get some enjoyment out of this.

She hurled the ball toward the bull's-eye plate that would send him plunging into the cold water, missing it by an inch. "Just so you know. I didn't aim to hit the target—yet. I have three more balls. One of them will find its mark. That's a promise. What I want to know is why."

"Why, what?" He knew she was wondering why he'd chosen her.

She pitched the ball toward him, this time a couple of feet off the target but inches from his body. "Wrong answer. You're an intelligent man. You know what I mean."

"Okay. The biggest contributor to the school fund was to be named either king or queen of the carnival. I was that person.

They told me I needed a queen to go with my king."

"Who?"

"Me, cuz."

Kim slanted her glance toward Maggie, who had approached. "You knew about this? Of course, you did. You probably made the banner without saying a word to me."

"I thought it would be a nice surprise. You and Zane will be featured in the newspaper tomorrow."

"Oh, I can hardly wait." She shifted her attention back to Zane. "Why me?"

He grinned. "Why not? I thought I would give you your fifteen minutes of fame."

"Wrong answer." She drilled the ball at the bull's-eye plate, striking it dead on. The bottom fell out of the platform Zane sat on, and he dropped into water that must have been chilled with ice cubes.

As he came up out of the water, he heard Jared say behind Kim, "Ah, Mrs.

Walters, I wanted to be the first one to dunk him."

"Sorry, Jared. I couldn't resist." She patted the boy's shoulder and walked away.

Chapter Ten

"You know how I feel about being in the limelight," Kim said when Anna hopped out of the truck at their house and raced for the stairs up to the second-floor gallery.

Zane climbed out of the front seat and slid in beside Kim in the back. "I wanted to surprise you. I thought being a teacher you would have grown out of that. You have to stand up in front of your class every day."

"They are nine-year-old kids. I think I can handle that."

"I never understood that about you. I

remember you were asked to run for student-council president, but you wouldn't because you had to give a speech in front of the whole student body. Everyone liked you. You would have won with no problem."

"I'm not comfortable with it. Wasn't then. I'm not now." Neither was she comfortable with Zane being mere inches from her in the cab. Or was she too comfortable? "You never answered me about why you picked me."

"I can't deny anymore there's something going on between us. This was a date—at least in my mind even if you didn't consider it that."

"I did."

"You did?"

She nodded then realized he probably couldn't see her in the dark cab. The light from the house didn't reach the truck. "Yes." Her voice squeaked, and she cringed, thankful he couldn't see that.

"Then why didn't you say it was?"

"Why didn't you?"

His laugh echoed through the cab. "We are a pair. We don't even know when we're dating."

"We did fifteen years ago."

"Everything was simple then."

"It was?"

"Okay, maybe not. But our perception of the past mellows some as time passes."

Maybe it had for him but not for her. The pain she'd gone through when he'd left town without a word to her was still engraved in her memories. She didn't want a repeat of that kind of heartache. Thoughts of the past fifteen years brought so much regret. "So that's why you never look back."

"What good does it do?"

"Remembering helps me not to repeat a mistake."

"Were we a mistake?"

She sucked in a ragged breath. "That's not an easy question to answer. What do you think?"

"I don't regret meeting you."

His tone indicated there was a but after that statement. "What do you regret?"

"I regret how I handled it. I regret the pain *both* of us suffered. How about you?"

"I regret marrying Scott on the rebound. Now that I look back at what happened after you left, I allowed myself to be talked into loving him because it was a good move for our family. Of course, now I know it wasn't. You know what they say about hindsight being twenty-twenty."

"I've heard rumors about Scott ever since I came back to Hope. But I know how gossip can be. I want to know from you what happened."

"Scott's family had financial problems that no one knew about. My husband took from my dad's business to try and shore up their investment company." Because it was dark in the truck and he couldn't see the anguish on her face, she felt safer telling him. She didn't share this with many people. "Dad thought Scott was the son he never had and trusted him with everything. That was a big mistake. One day

Scott was here and the next gone with his secretary. What a cliché. But then worse, we found out our family real-estate company was nearly broke."

"What did your father do?"

"He tried to hold the company together by selling off a lot of our land around the house. It wasn't enough. My ex-husband had helped himself to the money but had also made some bad decisions for the business. Then Mom got sick, and the medical bills completed what Scott had started. Everything came tumbling down, including my dad's health. It wasn't but six months after my mother passed away that he was diagnosed with Parkinson's disease." Telling him renewed the anguish those years had wrought. She'd lost so much. But strangely it felt right to tell him—to lct him know why she wouldn't commit herself again.

He covered her hand with his. "What did you do?"

"Finished my schooling and went to work while trying to raise my daughter and keep the family together as much as possible. But I don't regret having Anna. She is my life now."

"I remember how you wanted children."

"Why didn't you ever marry?" she finally asked the question that had bothered her for the past few weeks.

Rubbing his thumb across the back of her hand, he sighed. "Too busy working, learning the business."

"Why did you come back to Hope? I would think after what happened here, you would want to stay away."

"My dad was having problems. As much as there were times I wanted to turn my back on him in the long run I couldn't. Instead I decided to come home and try to help him. He is my only family."

She remembered the first time Maggie had told her that Zane was back in town. She'd literally panicked, and other than for work she hadn't left the house for a week, so afraid she would see him at any moment. "Still it had to be strange for you."

"My experiences here made me who I am today."

"And mine have for me." She angled toward him, the movement causing her hoop skirt to rise. She quickly held it down before it smothered her and Zane. "It seems our fathers have greatly affected our decisions over the years. As my dad gets worse with his Parkinson's disease, he'll need more care. That falls on me since I'm his only child."

"In my case, I'm glad I was the only child. I wouldn't want a sibling to have dealt with what I did growing up."

She and Zane had more in common than she realized. "Do you ever regret not having a family, children?"

"No, not really. Like I said, I wouldn't have had time for them like I should. That wouldn't have been right. I chose to go a different route. I help with the youth group. That gives me what I need."

"What's that?"

"The satisfaction from knowing that I'm helping the next generation, without being solely responsible for any one child. I saw what my father's drinking did to our family. He was never around. Although working all the time is different from drinking, the end result is the same. A kid with an absent father is not good."

"I know. I try to be both mother and father for Anna, but it's not easy. She never says anything, but I know she wonders about her dad. He left when she was a month old."

"I'm glad I haven't run into Scott. His treatment of you was…" His words spluttered to a stop. "Sorry, you probably don't need to hear that."

"Actually, you would have to get behind me and Dad. Although Dad wouldn't press charges, he has enumerated on a number of occasions what he would like to do to the man."

"Why didn't he press charges against Scott?"

"Mostly because we didn't have the proof we needed to make the charges stick. And also because Dad didn't want the Sommerfield name dragged through the gossip mill in Hope any more than it was when Scott left. His words, not mine."

Headlights illumined the inside of the truck as Maggie pulled up behind Zane. "That's my cue to leave. It's late."

Ten seconds later, a knock on the window produced a groan from Zane.

"It's only Maggie. Dad's going up the stairs."

Zane pushed open his door and climbed down to the ground, then swung around to help Kim exit as gracefully as she could in a wide skirt. Then he faced Maggie, the dim stream of light from the gallery illuminating her in shadows.

"Uncle Keith wants to know if y'all would like to come in."

"I have to go to Mobile tomorrow early. Long day. I'd better head home."

As he settled himself behind the steering wheel and rolled down the window, Kim asked, "What time on Monday will y'all start?"

"Check with your dad, and let me know

what works for you. My father is pretty flexible, and he'll be doing a lot of the work."

"I'll see you at church on Sunday and let you know then."

"Great. Is Anna going to stay for the youth group again?"

"Yes," Kim said as she backed away from the truck. At the bottom of the stairs she saw Maggie waiting for her, so she waved goodbye to Zane and followed her cousin up the steps. Before entering the house she asked Maggie, "Did Dad say anything?"

"No. He was actually preoccupied."

"About what?"

"If I had to guess, Ruth Coleman."

"Why? Did something happen tonight I don't know about?"

"I've never seen him enjoy himself so much in months—maybe years."

"Did he say anything about the kiss?" She hadn't wanted to upset her father any more than he already was because of the hurricane.

"He didn't but Ruth did. She thought the kiss was sweet and fifteen years in coming."

"Oh, that's probably not good. How did Dad respond?"

"He didn't. Not even one of his snorts."

"Really? Interesting. He isn't one for public display of affection."

Maggie put her hand on the door but didn't open it yet. "I caught him holding Ruth's hand."

"You did? Dad?"

"Yup. Thought I was hallucinating." With a smile on her face, Maggie entered the house.

"Where's Brady?" Kim asked as she followed.

"He went home with a friend to spend the night."

Kim crossed the game room toward the hallway, turning off lights as she went. "I think I'll check on Dad. I didn't get much chance tonight to talk with him. I want to make sure he's still okay about the renovations starting on Monday."

"Sure," Maggie said with a grin. "I know the truth. You want to gauge his real reaction to what happened on the stage."

In the corridor, Kim stopped and whirled toward her cousin behind her, the sweep of her hoop skirt nearly knocking over a small table. She shot her a conspiratorial smile. "I won't sleep a wink until I do."

As though she were the lady of the manor, Maggie strolled past her toward their room. "Quit fretting about it. You have to lead your own life, not worry about others."

"I don't. I—"

The look—both eyebrows raised—Maggie shot her before disappearing into the bedroom spoke volumes to Kim. Admittedly, Kim cared what her father thought. She owed him. He'd tried to fill in for Scott with Anna, to be there when Anna needed a father figure.

When Kim knocked on his door, she waited until he called out to come in. Still dressed in his Mad Hatter costume, minus the tall black hat, he sat in his chair, staring at the blank TV screen with a far-off expression on his face.

"Dad, are you all right?"

He slowly turned his head toward her. "I'm fine. Just thinking."

Kim took the chair at the desk. "About what?" she whispered, not sure she wanted to know.

"What do you think about Ruth? We've been friends for years but…" His voice fading, he looked away, biting his lower lip.

"I like her a lot. She will be a great mayor."

"I mean as…" He opened his mouth but no more words came out.

"What, Dad?"

He waved his hand in the air. "Nothing important. Working with her, I'm getting to know a different side of her."

"And you like what you see?"

His gaze zoomed in on her. "Yes. She has such passion about Hope and its people. It's refreshing. She makes me forget."

"Who? Mom?"

"No, the hurricane and its aftermath." He twisted his hands together. "What do you think your mother would feel if I—if I asked Ruth out after the mayor's race?"

"Why are you waiting?"

He lifted his shoulders in a shrug. "I don't know. It might complicate the campaign."

Kim stood. "Well, as far as Mom is concerned, I know she would want you to be happy. If that makes you happy, then you should go for it."

Her father picked up the remote and clicked on the TV. "I just might do that." When she didn't leave right away, he asked, "Did you need me for something?"

When she'd walked in, she'd been sure her father would make a few comments about what had happened on the stage. Now that he hadn't, she brought up another reason for being there. "Zane wants to start Monday. We talked about that a few days ago. Is that still okay with you?"

"Yes. The quicker I can get this house back in order, the quicker I can get my life back in order. I'll be at Ruth's a good part of the day. In fact, I'll have you drop me off on the way to school and pick me up when you get through. If my plans change, I'll call you at school."

"Since I'll be going up to school to-morrow and Sunday afternoon to get my room in order, I won't stay extra long on Monday. I'll let Zane know they can start anytime after seven-thirty."

"Fine," her dad murmured, already lost in the show he'd found to watch.

Kim let herself out of the room and paused in the hallway. She'd gotten a glimpse of the man her father used to be before the hurricane—calmer, more in control. She wanted that man back for good.

Kim stood with Zane's father in the entrance to her old bedroom before the storm, the odor of paint hanging in the air. "Mr. Davidson, I can't thank you enough for the work you've done on my room. After the hurricane, I wasn't even sure if we would be able to use this area again. Naomi did a number on it."

"Call me Tom. After all, we've been painting together. I think that calls for first names, don't ya?" He backed away from caulking the tall window that over-looked the back of the property.

In the past couple of weeks as Tom had worked on her bedroom, their relationship had changed, especially when she came home from school and helped him any way she could from holding something in place to painting the room over the past few nights. She skimmed the length of her. "One day I'm going to get the hang of it and not end up with so much paint on me."

He wheeled around toward her. "I'd say those clothes are heading for the trash."

"That's why I wore really old pants and

shirt. They should have been in the trash, anyway."

"Once I paint the windowsill and clear all my things out of here, your room will be ready for you to move back in."

"Today?"

He nodded. "And your dad's room will be finished by the first of the week."

Joy flowed through her, lifting her spirits. "Thank you, Tom. This means so much to us."

Zane's dad ducked his head and squatted by his toolbox. "Just part of the job," he mumbled.

"Your work is beautiful. I didn't think the crown molding or these hardwood floors could be restored."

He straightened. "I'll be starting on the last three rooms after I finish your dad's." His gaze fell on something behind her.

Kim whirled around and nearly collided with Zane. Seeing him reminded her of their appointment for the neighborhood sweeps. She'd gotten so preoccupied by the painting, she'd lost track of time. "I'm late, aren't I?"

"Yup. I'm here to pick you up, and I don't think you'll want to go around the neighborhoods with—" he brushed his fingers along the left side of her head "—a streak of green paint in your hair. It matches your clothes, but since you'll be seeing some of your kids' parents, you might want to wash it out and change."

"If you want, you can go ahead, and I'll meet up with you when I get ready."

"Nah. I'll wait for you. There's no set time we have to do this today. I need to check with Dad about his schedule, anyway."

Kim rushed toward the bedroom she was using and gathered her clothes. Then she headed toward the bathroom for a shower. Fifteen minutes later, she presented herself at the entrance of her renovated bedroom. "I'm ready."

Zane finished helping his dad fold the drop cloth, then made his way to Kim. Over his shoulder he said to his dad, "I'll be able to help you on Monday. My other projects are coming along nicely. Also I'm pulling Beau to work with you."

"Whatever you can spare," Tom said as he continued to clean up the mess.

Kim descended the staircase to the first floor. "I'll get to move into my own bedroom tonight. I feel like celebrating."

Opening the front door, Zane stood back and let her go out onto the veranda. "After we do our neighborhood sweep, I'll spring for ice cream at Sweet Tooth."

Memories of all the times they had gone to Sweet Tooth to celebrate something special inundated Kim. A warning went up: *you're getting in over your head. Say no.* Instead, she replied, "I'm already thinking about a double scoop of Pecan Clusters."

"Why does that not surprise me?"

"Because my tastes have not changed. Caramel and nuts are a must in my ice cream."

Zane reached for his passenger door on

his truck. "My favorite is still Chocolate Supreme."

"If we continue to talk about this, I'm going to have to stop on the way there and back. That wouldn't do. I've worked hard to keep the pounds off."

"And all that hard work has paid off," Zane said, giving her a wink and starting the engine. As he drove, he told her, "Cody heard back from the national headquarters about my proposition concerning building and repairing houses in disaster areas." He took a corner, and didn't say anything.

"And?"

"We're moving forward. They are very interested. In a few weeks, I'll be flying to Nashville to meet with their whole board. In the meantime, I have to gather some info and send it to them."

"Do you need any help?"

"Someone to type it all up. Susan can but she's—"

"Consider me that person."

"Are you sure? I wouldn't impose, but

I'd promised Susan a few days off after the school was completed."

"I want to do this." She angled toward him. "Have you seen the extra work your dad is doing?"

"Every morning he gets up excited to go to work. I think what he enjoys the most is restoring something old. This may be another area my company can expand into."

"Just how big is your operation?"

"I have three full offices—New Orleans, Hope and Mobile. I'm thinking of opening one in Pensacola next year. I'll probably wait until I see what happens with the foundation."

"How do you keep it all straight?"

"Good people in my offices."

"That was my father's problem. He didn't have good people working for him. Besides Scott, there were a couple of others that made some bad decisions, too."

"I'm sorry to hear that." Kindness sculpted his features.

"You really mean that, even after what my dad did?"

He nodded. "It didn't happen overnight. There were many years I was so angry at your dad that I think I would have punched him in the face if I'd met him on the street. Now you see why I didn't come home."

"I appreciate your restraint."

Zane pulled up to the curb of the first street they had been assigned and parked. Locking gazes with her, he said, "There were other reasons I stayed away, but I did come back once."

"When?"

"About a year after I left. I came back because I decided to fight for you."

Surprise held her immobile. "I never saw you."

"I know. I discovered you had recently gotten engaged to Scott Walters and were getting married a few months later."

"But you should have said something."

"Why? Would that have made a difference? Scott had your family's stamp of approval. And I still didn't feel real good about myself."

"But you were—"

He placed two fingers over her mouth. "Don't say anything. It doesn't change what happened. You had made your choice, and frankly at the time I thought Scott would be just what you needed."

She pulled away from his touch. "I love how everyone tries to run my life. First my father then you. And look how well his choice turned out for me." Flinging the door open, she turned away and climbed from the cab. "Next time I would like someone to consult me before making decisions for me. I'll take the right side of the street. You take the left."

By the time she'd covered her side except for the last house of one of her students, her anger subsided to a dull throb behind her eyes. Grace Langley lived here with her father, a man too proud to ask for help. She knocked on the door of the small trailer parked in the driveway. Not much was left of their home except the foundation. The only thing that had been done was most of the debris had been cleared from the yard and the concrete foundation. Strangely the garage still stood. She rapped on the metal door again.

When she stepped away from the trailer, a tall, muscular man she'd only met once, on the first day of school, appeared from the garage. He stopped a few feet from her. "What do ya want?"

"I'm Kim Walters, Grace's teacher."

"Yeah, I know. Is something wrong at school? With Grace?"

Trying to ignore his glare, she forced a smile. "Grace is a delight."

"Then good day." He pivoted.

"Mr. Langley, I'm here about supporting Ruth Coleman for mayor."

He peered over his shoulder, that glare firmly in place. "I don't vote. Why bother? Nothing ever changes."

"But, Mr. Langley, Ruth will have monthly meetings with the townspeople who—"

Laughter roared from the man. "That's

a good one. Where? City hall? How ya gonna fit everyone in there? Leave us alone. I have enough to deal with."

He continued striding toward the garage and his daughter who stood in its door-way. Grace waved to her, but the second her father entered the garage, he shut the door, the sound reverberating through the air.

Zane came up to her. "I gather he won't be voting for Ruth."

"He won't be voting for either candidate." Kim marched toward the entrance he'd disappeared through.

Zane kept pace with her. "I don't think he'll listen to anything about the mayor's race."

"I totally agree. Now I am approaching him as Grace's teacher."

"I'm coming with you. He didn't sound too hospitable."

"Then don't say anything." Kim knocked on the garage door.

Grace opened it. "Hi, Mrs. Walters."

"Who is it?" Mr. Langley shouted from the back.

"My teacher." The little girl stepped to the side to let Kim into the building.

"What are you doing?" Mr. Langley came around a partition. "I thought I made myself clear. I am not voting."

In the dim light in the garage with only one window on the side of it, Kim surveyed what had to be their living space—not the trailer parked in the driveway. She quickly skimmed over the bottle of whiskey sitting on a card table, probably where they ate. The overriding odor in the place was a musty scent she'd remembered permeating her downstairs after the water had receded. "I'm not here as a campaign worker now. I'm here as Grace's teacher."

"Snooping. Get out!"

"Daddy!" Grace said, tears crowding her voice.

The burly man swung his attention to his daughter. The glare that Kim had thought was permanently etched onto his face softened. "Sugar, we've got a lot to do.

She told me ya were doing okay. That's all I need to know." When he looked again at Kim, the scowl returned. "Isn't that right, lady?"

"Yes, Grace is a wonderful—"

The man charged toward the door and thrust it open. "Bye."

Kim took a step toward Mr. Langley, but before she could take another, Zane clasped her hand, halting her progress, and said, "Thank you for your time."

Kim shook off his hand and strode out of the garage, not stopping until she was near the trailer. Then she rounded on Zane. "What were you doing back there? Playing some macho male or something with me, not him. You thanked him for his time."

"Being confrontational with Mr. Langley won't get you what you want. That scene in there was played out several times in my childhood. I know you saw the bottle on the table and you couldn't have missed the liquor on the man's breath."

"But what about Grace? I should report him or something."

"To whom? He's given her a roof over her head. She doesn't appear to be abused. She wasn't scared of her father. Have you ever seen any signs of abuse?"

"Well, no, but she wears the same clothes over and over."

"Are they clean?"

"Yes. So is Grace."

"It isn't against the law to be poor."

She settled her balled hands on her waist. "But he won't accept any help, not even free lunches." She gestured toward the trailer. "Why isn't he using this to live in?"

"I can't answer that. But there is a For Sale sign on the front of it."

"There is?" She rounded the trailer and found the sign in red and white.

"I think they need money, and he's selling what he can."

"How did it survive the hurricane? Look what happened to his house. Probably the only reason his garage is still standing is because it was behind the house and set back some."

"I don't know. Maybe it wasn't parked here. What does he do?"

"He's a charter-boat captain. Business right now is lousy."

"It's gonna take a while for the tourist industry to make a comeback. So what's the man doing for money?"

"Grace hasn't said much about her dad, and he hasn't come to any parent meetings. I met him at the first day of school. That's all." Throwing one last look at the garage, Kim started toward Zane's truck at the other end of the block. "How did it go for you?"

"I got a lot of interest in Ruth for mayor. How about you?"

"Five yesses, two nos and Mr. Langley."

"We've got six more streets to cover. Maybe we can turn things in Ruth's favor."

"Yes," Kim mumbled as she got into the truck, her thoughts on Grace. The girl had always been upbeat with her classmates, but Kim had glimpsed a hint of sadness in her eyes tonight. She wished she had money to purchase the trailer. At one time, her family could have helped. Frustration bubbled in the pit of her stomach.

Chapter Eleven

Sitting across from Kim in a booth at Sweet Tooth, Zane took a lick of his Chocolate Supreme ice cream cone. "After all the walking we did this afternoon, this hits the spot."

Kim picked up a napkin and leaned toward him, swiping it across his mouth. "Chocolate."

Her gesture caused a chain reaction in him: increased pulse rate, a tightness in his chest, a rise in his body temperature. Just like when he'd been nineteen. He tried to shut down those physical responses. He didn't live in the past, and he certainly didn't want to repeat it. But more and more he found himself thinking about Kim, what she was thinking, doing.

"I know you were upset about Mr. Langley. How about the other parents you talked with? Did it go okay with them?"

"Yes. The kids were happy to see me outside of school, and it's always easier to talk with the parents in an informal setting." Her forehead scrunched. "But I wish there was something I could do for Grace and her father."

"He reminds me of my father. He wouldn't let anyone help him, either. He had to hit rock bottom before he accepted help seven months ago." The vision of the For Sale sign on the trailer played across his mind, flashing in and out.

"Do you think Mr. Langley is an alcoholic?"

"All I can say is he has been drinking. That doesn't necessarily mean he's an alcoholic, but if he keeps turning to alcohol to blot out his problems, he will be. That's how it started with my dad."

"I don't want Grace to go through what you went through."

"Neither do I." He popped the last bite of his cone into his mouth and chewed, trying to decide what to do, if anything.

"Do you know anyone looking for a boat captain?"

"Hmm. I'll have to check around. When we get closer to summer, his business should pick up some. What if he moved his boat to one of the larger piers like in Gulfport or Biloxi?"

"I have the feeling the rent is high for a berth at those piers."

Zane wiped his mouth with his napkin then balled it up. "I could use a smaller trailer for a certain work site. I'll pay the man a visit and see what he's asking for it. But first I'm gonna call a friend in New Orleans. He might be able to give him a job."

"Doing what?"

"Ferrying boats. My friend owns the business where I bought my sailboat. Sometimes customers have to have someone take the boat they bought to another location. He might be able to use Mr. Langley. I'll have to check out people he's worked with. I can't recommend someone who could hurt my friend's business."

"No, you can't, but if you could help Mr. Langley, that would be great. He hasn't accepted anything I suggested."

"I have one advantage over you."

"What?" She scooped up the last of her Pecan Clusters and slid the spoon into her mouth.

For a few seconds he sat there transfixed as she ate her ice cream, until he realized she was waiting for an answer. "I'm male. He may be one of those guys who doesn't respond well to women. Do you know what happened to his wife?"

"All I know is that she died a few years back when Grace was in kindergarten. I talked to her teacher, and she said it was rough on Mr. Langley and Grace. The child didn't come to school for a month."

Zane's past crept back into his thoughts. When his mother had left his dad and him, he'd refused to go to school for weeks. He kept waiting for his mom to come back home. She never did. "I'll see what I can do."

Kim smiled. "That means a lot to me. And if the fact that you are a man helps to reach Mr. Langley, that's fine by me."

Looking at the sparkle in her eyes made him think of staring at the blue Gulf water with the sun shining on its surface while he sailed. "I'll let you know what happens. Are you ready? I know you can't wait to get back home and move back into your bedroom."

She scooted back her chair and rose. "Ice cream is about the only thing that can entice me to put that off for a while." Cocking her head to one side, she pinned him beneath an assessing look. "Are you doing anything tonight?"

"I'm helping a…friend."

"Oh." She slung the strap of her purse over her shoulder and started for the exit.

He bit the inside of his cheek to keep from laughing at the crestfallen expression on Kim's face. As she walked out of the Sweet Tooth, he quickened his pace after her, catching up with her at the parking lot next to the building.

As his engine roared to life, he threw her a sideways glance. "You coming to church tomorrow?"

"Dad wants to, so, yes, I'll be bringing him and Anna."

Five minutes later, Zane stopped in the back of Bienville near the staircase to the upstairs gallery and switched off the engine, then put his hand on the door handle.

"You don't have to walk me to my door. I'm sure you need to get moving if you're going to help that friend." She descended from the truck and strolled toward her home. When he followed, she glanced back with a question in her eyes. At the bottom step, she spun around, her hand clutching the railing. "I'm a big girl. I can find my own way to my house."

"I know. But I have to come in if I'm going to help you move your furniture."

"*I'm* the friend you're going to help?"

He smiled when the realization dawned on her pretty face. "Of course. You don't think I'll let you do it by yourself. Even with Brady and Maggie, it will be hard. You've got some big pieces." He backed away. "Unless you don't want my help."

"Yes. Yes. I'm not like Mr. Langley. I will accept help when I need it."

"Really?"

She shot him a gaze full of mockery. "I accepted your help with the house, didn't I?"

"Not until you demanded doing something for me in return."

Square in the middle of the staircase, she blocked his path. "And what is your point?"

He laughed. "That you're as stubborn as you were in high school. You might not be as extreme as Mr. Langley, but you do have trouble accepting help from others."

She wheeled around and stomped up the steps to the gallery. At the back door, she thrust it open and entered.

Women! Zane blew out a long breath and went into the game room. Kim was talking to Maggie, who was making dinner.

"I got some good comments about Ruth running in the area I canvassed." Maggie put a casserole into the oven.

"I did, too. And I only had one person practically throw me off his property." Kim washed her hands at the sink then began setting the table.

"Who?"

"Mr. Langley, the father of one of my students. He sees no reason to vote for mayor."

"That's a shame, but I encountered a few like that, too. They are struggling and have lost hope." Maggie turned toward Zane. "Are you staying for dinner?"

Zane peered at Kim.

"Yes, he is. He's *helping* me move my furniture back into my bedroom."

"Good. I didn't want to eat alone. Anna is eating at Polly's. Brady is at a friend's, too."

"Where's Dad?"

"He just called five minutes ago and said he'd be eating at Ruth's tonight. I'd already started the Mexican chicken casserole so I decided to finish it, and we can have it again for leftovers."

The spices and chicken smells oozed out of the oven and infused the room, reminding Zane that he'd forgotten to eat lunch again. A bagel and an ice-cream cone weren't exactly a healthy diet. "As hungry as I am, you might not have any leftovers. Do you want to move some of the furniture now while the casserole is cooking?"

"Sounds like a plan to me." Kim set the three glasses on the place mats on the table.

Maggie filled a kettle with water. "I'll be a minute. I want to make the iced tea so it will be ready when we eat."

At the entrance into the bedroom, Kim paused and sucked in a raspy breath. Zane came up behind her and whistled.

The empty room looked spotless, and Zane marveled at the difference from when Kim and he were there four hours before. "Dad did a great job."

"He polished the hardwood floor. There's not a speck of dust anywhere. He didn't have to do that."

Zane's throat closed. He coughed to clear it. "That's his way of apologizing."

"For what?"

"For not telling you anything fifteen years ago—not where I went or why. He's trying to right any wrongs he feels he's made in the past."

"But you told him not to."

"Yeah, and that was one of the few times my dad ever listened to me." He shook his head. "He told me the other day he'd made a mistake about you."

Kim turned to leave, but Zane held his position in the doorway. "The furniture is in the room down the hall."

"I know."

"Well, we…" Her voice cracked on the last word, and she lifted huge eyes to his. Her teeth worried her bottom lip.

The need to kiss her overwhelmed him.

Ever since two weeks ago when he'd kissed her onstage, he'd wanted to again. He'd forgotten how good he felt when he did. She made him feel like he was the only one.

But he knew differently.

She'd married Scott, not a year after he left. And because of that relationship, she held a part of herself back from others, from him.

She moved toward him as though to push him back to let herself out into the corridor. But a half a foot from him, she came to a stop, lifted her hand and touched his chest. "I'll admit I have a hard time accepting help from others. I've always been the fixer around here, the person others came to. When I can't make something better, it makes me feel like I've failed."

He cupped her jaw. "So you feel you have to have all the right answers all the time?"

"Is that the way it seems?"

With a nod, he slid his palm around to the back of her head and tugged her close.

"You think that asking for help means you're not strong, you're not in control. Your dad isn't the only one who feels that way."

"There's nothing wrong with wanting to be in control of your own life."

"Control. That's an illusion." He snapped his fingers. "Life can change at any second."

"Yeah, the hurricane brought that home to me."

"It did to a lot of people."

"I know."

The resignation in her voice touched him. She was trying to make sense of something that couldn't always be explained in a neat little package. He roped her against him, her head tilted up toward his. "We've done a lot today. Why don't I come over tomorrow and help you move everything back into here? Rest tonight."

"No, I want to put my room in order. I'm tired, but I can't rest until it is done."

His concern grew as he stared at her. She was pushing herself too hard. "Okay, then let me call Dad and have him come back and help me while you rest."

"I can't ask—"

"Shh. You're not asking. I am. He won't mind. He'll get a kick out of helping put the room together. You have some beautiful pieces of old furniture."

"They're called antiques. They have been in the family for a long time. A lot of history."

Tightening his arms about her, he dipped his head toward her and settled his mouth over hers, pouring his growing feelings for her into the kiss. She responded, embracing him as though she wasn't going to let him go.

A cough behind him alerted him they weren't alone. He reluctantly lessened the pressure of his lips on hers until they parted. Slowly he shifted partway to find Maggie standing in the hallway with amusement on her face.

"I could go back and bake a cake if y'all want."

A twinkle in Maggie's eyes brought

forth a chuckle as he released Kim. "Why don't you two do that while I get Dad over here to help me?"

Maggie's forehead creased. "You really want one?"

"That or go watch TV or knit or whatever you want. In other words, you two aren't needed."

Maggie's shoulders slumped. "And I was so looking forward to lifting heavy pieces of furniture. But if you insist, I think I can manage to knit. And, Kim, we haven't talked about what we're going to wear to Kathleen and Gideon's wedding next Saturday."

When Maggie returned to the game room, Zane withdrew his cell, made a call to his dad then pocketed his phone. "Tell me where you want everything," he told Kim, "then go do something else."

"You're mighty bossy."

"I've gotten in the habit since I run my own company. It's one of those necessary things an owner has to do."

She pivoted back into her room and

pointed along the east wall. "My bed goes there with the bedside tables. My dresser over there and the armoire across from it." When she finished showing him where she wanted her furniture, she thought for a moment then frowned. "Maybe I should stay in here, at least, just in case you need me."

Zane went through the list of furniture and where she wanted it. "Is that right?"

"Yes, but—"

He took her hand and headed for the game room. "Relax. Stop worrying. When Dad arrives send him to me. I'm going to start with the smaller pieces."

"How about dinner?"

"Call us. We'll come when it's ready. I don't want you stepping foot in your bedroom until we've got it set up. Okay?"

"Fine. But I'm declaring right now, I don't like this."

He tweaked her nose. "I know. Live dangerously. Give control over to me."

Maggie leaned around Zane sitting between her and Kim. "You know it's very telling that Uncle Keith is sitting up on the front pew with Ruth as if he is a member of the bride's family."

Kim found her father, looking handsome in his black suit and sky-blue silk tie. The smile on his face brought a tear to her eye. She quickly blinked it away. "I was surprised when he told me last night after he escorted Ruth to the rehearsal dinner."

"Yeah, I know they're spending a lot of time together on the campaign, but—"

Zane bent toward them conversing across his lap. "Ladies, I think the wedding is about to start."

Kim straightened at the same time Maggie did and murmured, "Spoilsport."

"Someone's gotta keep order in the masses."

The music started, and one of Kathleen's cousins, Sally, stood at the front and began singing "I Don't Want to Miss a Thing." Zane covered Kim's hand with his. The warmth of his palm only added to the moment as Sally finished the song and the "Wedding March" started.

The congregation rose. Zane kept her hand within his and tugged her close as Kathleen glided down the aisle toward Gideon. Dressed in an ivory silk suit, Kathleen looked beautiful. More tears lodged in Kim's throat. She usually cried at weddings, though she was never sure why.

When they took their seats again, Kim fixed her attention on the couple in front of the pastor at Hope Community Church, but she couldn't really focus on the wedding or what was being said. She tried to figure out why she cried at a happy occasion because Kathleen and Gideon were very much in love. Anyone looking at them could see that.

Then toward the end of the ceremony, the reason came to her. She'd had such high hopes for her own marriage, and they had been dashed within the first six months she was Scott's wife. They had met their families' expectations for them but not their own. If she'd known that while walking down the aisle, she would have hiked up her skirt and hightailed it in the opposite direction. She hadn't, and the repercussions were still affecting her today, fourteen years later.

"Ready to go to the reception?" Zane whispered in her ear when she finally noticed people beginning to leave the church.

She gave him a nod, tightly clamping a lid on her emotions. She was happy for Kathleen and Gideon. This was their day. *I refuse to think about my situation.*

"I'm going ahead. I'll grab a table for us." Maggie plowed through the crowd.

In the reception hall, Kim spied Maggie waving to them across the room. Brady and Anna darted forward toward the area where the kids were hanging out. Cody broke from the throng and grabbed a chair next to Kim. Zane's secretary, Susan, saw them and made a beeline toward the table.

"Did they invite everyone in town?" she said, sinking into a seat across from Kim.

"Boss, I hardly see you dressed up. You look good."

Kim glanced at Zane in a navy blue suit that highlighted the blue of his eyes. She had to totally agree with Susan's assessment, but she would never tell Zane. She was already caring for him too much. This wedding only reconfirmed her need to keep her distance. As if that was going to happen with him and his dad renovating Bienville.

After a few more guests sat at the table and filled every seat, Maggie said, "Kim, I forgot to tell you a couple of Sundays ago I volunteered you for clean-up duty after the reception."

"How could you forget to tell me something like that?"

Maggie offered Kim a sheepish grin. "If I remember correctly, that was the day you were setting up your classroom. With all that's happened, it slipped my mind. Sorry. You don't have to if you don't want to."

"I can do it," she said, slanting a look at Zane. "That is if you don't mind waiting."

"I'll help, too. Then it'll get done quicker."

"I can stay," Susan said. "I don't have anything to do after this."

"Me, too," Cody added.

Kim thanked everyone for their help. "With all of you, we won't take long at all."

"Do you see Dad with Ruth?" she asked Cody. "He's hanging on her every word."

Cody chuckled. "That doesn't surprise me. He's had a lot to say about the campaign and her. I didn't realize he'd been a councilman at one time. He sounds like he loved it. I've encouraged him to get involved again."

"So that's why he's thinking of running for the council next year."

Zane slid his arm along the back of Kim's chair. "They would make a dynamite pair running the town."

Kim swung her gaze to him. "You mean that?"

He stared at her. "I wouldn't have said it if I hadn't meant it."

The people around them faded from Kim's consciousness. The electric connection between them intensified, his face close to hers, their breath mingling.

Maggie elbowed Zane. "Gideon is removing the garter. You should see if you can catch it."

He shook his head. "No way."

But when Miss Alice and Ruth began recruiting the single men to come up, Kim's dad appeared at the table. "Come on, Cody and Zane. That includes you."

"How about you, Dad?" Kim asked him.

"Ruth has threatened me within an inch of my life if I'm not in the front of the group. But I'm not standing alone. If I have to, you two can, too."

Groaning, Zane rose, bent down and whispered to Kim, "You're gonna owe me."

Five minutes later when Gideon shot the garter into the cluster of single males in the middle of the large room, Kim tried to follow its projection but lost sight of it as a few men fled the garter while a couple dove for it. Her father didn't move, and it landed square in the middle of his chest. With his slow reflexes, he barely caught it before it fell to the floor.

Ruth laughed and kissed Kim's dad on the cheek. Bright red flooded his face.

As Zane and Cody made their way back to the table, Kim's dad said, "Now it's the single women's time. Come on. I want every female over the age of eighteen up here." He looked straight at Maggie then Kim.

Zane stopped behind Kim's chair. "Let me help you up."

"Oh, that's okay. I'm fine right here."

He scooted the seat back from the table. "Give me the pleasure of escorting you up there."

Kim's father snapped the garter on the upper arm of his jacket then honed in on Kim. Standing, she ignored Zane and cut the distance between her and the single women gathering. Kim positioned herself between Susan and Maggie.

Kathleen turned her back on the group of women and tossed the bouquet over her head. It came right for Kim. She stepped back as Susan jumped in the air and caught the flowers.

Maggie sidled closer to Kim. "I noticed you got out of the way of the bouquet. I thought you and Zane were getting serious."

"What gave you that idea?"

"Oh, let me see—" her cousin tapped her chin with a finger "—the kiss last Saturday night or the one on the stage. That didn't look like two people who weren't interested in each other."

"Okay, I care about him. Is that what you want to hear?"

"Why so defensive?"

"Because I don't want to care about Zane. My track record with men isn't too good, and he was one of the men."

"Then you'd better stop kissing him because, honey, you're only getting yourself in deeper each time you do. You've never been a woman who does anything lightly, and that includes kissing."

Over Maggie's shoulder Kim noticed Zane heading for them. "Shh. He's coming."

But what her cousin said never left Kim throughout the rest of the reception. By the time she stayed to clean up with Maggie, Cody, Susan and Zane, she felt more confused than ever. How could she trust her judgment after what had happened between them?

As the reception hall began to look like it had before the wedding, Kim slipped out of the room and went into the sanctuary. Taking a seat on the back pew, she stared at the cross hanging above the altar. *I need help, Lord. I don't know what to do. Can You help me?*

"Another week and your upstairs will be finished," Zane said as he applied the last of the polyurethane finish to the hardwood floor in her dad's bedroom, backing himself out of the doorway. He peered up at Kim a few feet behind him and noted the wet clothes and hair. "Is it raining?"

"Yes, it started about five minutes ago. Just enough to get me wet while I ran to the house."

"It'll probably take a little longer for this to dry, then, but your dad should be back in his own room in a few days."

"I'm sure he'll be happy to hear that."

Zane rose, putting the roller on top of the empty can of finish. "Maggie told me he went to see Cody today. How's the counseling going?"

"Each week he's getting better."

"Where is he?" Though Keith Sommerfield no longer left the room when Zane appeared, they weren't friends, either. When around the man, Zane felt like he was constantly being assessed, and he wasn't quite sure what Kim's father thought of him now.

"He's in the game room. He's telling the kids about how successful the neighborhood sweeps were a few weekends ago.

Next he's going to ask me to pat him on the back."

"I don't know about you, but he deserves it. The election is next Tuesday, and Ruth is way ahead of her opponent in the poll the newspaper ran."

Kim grinned. "Yeah, I know. He told me that all the way to Cody's office."

Thunder rumbled in the air. Zane glanced toward the open window across the room. "I'm glad there's an overhang, but we'll need to keep track of the direction the rain is falling. I'd rather not have to walk on the floor until it's dry, but if it changes, I might have to close that window."

"I didn't realize it was going to rain today. It was sunny when I took Dad then went grocery shopping. Now that our roof is fixed, I'm not as obsessed with the weather."

"Living dangerously?"

"Yup. Left the house without an umbrella."

Zane sniffed the air. "Ah, coffee. Maggie must be making some more."

Kim scanned the hallway. "Where's your dad?"

"AA meeting. He'd planned to come back after it if it's not too late. Sometimes they go out to eat afterward."

"I feel guilty. He's here when I leave in the morning for school and stays until it's dark. I can't get him to stay for dinner. A few times he's taken some food with him."

"And I have appreciated it. Delicious." Zane led Kim toward the game room.

"The first room I want renovated downstairs is the kitchen."

"Then that's what Dad and I will tackle first."

"When are you leaving for Nashville and the meeting with the Christian Assistance Coalition?"

"Wednesday." Maggie poured some coffee into a mug and turned toward Zane. He walked straight for it, arm outstretched. "I'm in your debt, Maggie."

"No, the fact that I'm getting my own

bedroom back far outweighs a cup of coffee."

"Not when you didn't have your quota for the day."

"Where's Dad?" Kim chimed in to ask of Maggie. "I didn't see him go to his room."

"Anna is on the gallery watching the storm move in. He went out to see if she was all right."

"Is something wrong?" Kim started for the door to the outside.

"She came home from Polly's a little while ago and didn't say much. Just went out onto the gallery."

"She must be in front since I didn't see her when I got home."

Zane hung back with Maggie, sipping his coffee. "I'll stay here and wheedle a dinner invitation out of Maggie."

As Kim left the house, Keith entered, his gaze pausing on Zane for a few extra seconds before he grinned at Maggie. "I could use a cup of coffee. It's getting cold out there. The wind is whipping up, but I can't get Anna to come in."

Maggie stood in front of a cabinet selecting some spices, and Zane moved to the pot to fill a mug. He held it out to Keith.

Keith stared at the coffee, not making a move to take it. Zane wasn't sure what he should do and started to place it on the counter and join Kim on the gallery when Keith finally reached for the mug, his hand shaking.

Keith took it, cradling it between his hands. "It's been a long day. I guess I'm more tired than I thought."

"Other than a few finishing touches, your room is done. Once the floor dries completely, you'll be able to move back into it."

"I know a young man who'll be happy to have his bedroom back to himself." Keith eased down into a lounge chair.

"Uncle Keith, Brady has enjoyed sharing his room with you."

Keith snorted. "Poppycock." After

taking a sip of his drink, he swept his arm toward the couch and looked at Zane. "Rest. You've been working since early this morning. What are y'all going to do next?" He leaned forward and glanced around. "Where is your dad?"

Zane was grateful for the sturdy sofa, because the shock almost knocked him over. He drank some of his coffee to cover it as much as possible.

"He'll be back soon. He had a meeting to go to."

"I'm impressed with his work. I told him that yesterday."

"He thinks this place is beautiful. Dad loves old buildings."

"So do I. There's so much history in them."

Lightning flashed followed by a boom ripping through the air. Zane flinched and gripped his mug tighter. "The storm is getting worse."

Keith grinned. "But we don't have any leaks. That's something to celebrate." Relaxing back, he crossed his legs and asked again, "What are y'all going to do next?"

"Finish up with the guest bedroom then move to the downstairs."

Out on the gallery, Anna yelped at the sound of thunder and jumped back from the railing.

Kim put her hand on her daughter's shoulder. "You're usually not this quiet, especially if something is bothering you. Hon, what's going on?"

Anna didn't say anything.

Kim searched the darkness, trying to discern her expression, but the shadows hid it. "Maybe I can help you." A streak of lightning lit the encroaching night, brought on early by the black clouds of the storm. Kim glimpsed Anna's dropped head, her hair falling forward to conceal her face. She gently squeezed her daughter's shoulder. "You're scaring me. What has happened?"

"Nothing. I'm fine," she mumbled in a voice that denied each word.

She didn't have to see Anna's face to realize tears were near the surface. "Did you have a fight with Polly?"

"No."

"Someone else?"

Silence greeted that question.

Kim wanted to fight her child's battles for her but knew she couldn't—that in the long run that wasn't the best thing for Anna. She needed to learn to do it herself. But that didn't mean Kim couldn't support her every step of the way. "Sometimes talking about a problem helps you to see a solution."

Her child's sigh overrode the noises of the rain beating down on the house. "A couple of girls came over to Polly's to play today. One was Lily."

That right there said a lot. Lily was the only cousin whom Anna couldn't get along with. "What happened?"

"I try to put up with her because Polly likes her, but she's mean."

"As hard as this can be at times, you need to ignore what she says."

"Polly asked about when I'd get my old bedroom back. That led to talk about the house being fixed up by Zane. One of the girls said we were lucky to get him to do the work. Her dad loved what he did for them. Lily wanted to know when I'd finally get a daddy. She said that my father didn't want me and left. Maybe Zane would, too."

Kim heard each of her daughter's words but couldn't respond. Instead, they thrust her back to the day that Scott had left. Or rather the day he'd left a note on the refrigerator telling her he was divorcing her and his lawyer would contact her about it. She visualized the words on the paper and the feelings she'd experienced then washed over her again—the shock, the grief, the anger, the humiliation of her husband walking out on her.

"Mom?"

Her daughter's voice pulled her back to the present, and she realized she'd gripped Anna's shoulder so tightly her hand ached. She loosened her hold and stepped around in front of her daughter. "Did she say anything else?"

"She told me she'd overheard her mother and grandmother talking about how sad it was that my father didn't want children. That was why he left you. Am I the reason?"

A bolt of lightning in the distance illuminated Anna's face enough for Kim to see the sad droop to her eyes, the shiny gleam in them. She pulled her against her and encircled her in her embrace. "I'm the reason, not you. Never you."

"But he left right after I was born," her daughter said, pressed against Kim's chest.

"He didn't love me. He had someone else." She didn't want to explain the whole mess to Anna, at least not until she was older.

"But he never calls me, never comes to see me."

If she could get hold of Scott right now, she'd give him a piece of her mind for putting her in this situation. "He didn't want children. That's true, but it really had nothing to do with you. He wanted to be free of any kind of obligation, and children are a big obligation. When I became pregnant with you, I'd hoped he would change his mind because I wanted you very much. More than I can say in words." Kim leaned back and framed Anna's face in her hands. "I love you more than you can imagine. Papa Keith loves you. Maggie and even Brady. We're your family."

"I've been afraid to talk about him. I know when I've said something about him, it has bothered you. But I have questions."

Zane's words about forgiveness and letting go of the past inundated Kim. Because she hadn't, her daughter had been afraid to talk to her. That wasn't right. *Please, Lord, help me to let this anger toward Scott go. I'm too tired to fight it anymore.*

"I'm sorry, hon. You should never be afraid to ask me a question. What do you want to know? I'll tell you what I can. You have a right to know."

"Where's Daddy?"

"I don't know. Even when his mother lived here, she wouldn't say anything about where Scott was. No one in the family will say anything. Any connection I've had with your daddy is through a lawyer."

"Is that why they don't do much with me?"

"You go over to see them on holidays." The light came on in the bedroom with the window right behind them, giving Kim enough glow to see Anna's expression— one of a child in pain. She felt responsible.

"But they never really say anything to me."

Kim clenched her jaws together until she could control what she said to her daughter. "They didn't talk to you? Why didn't you tell me?"

"They did. But like I was a stranger." Her shoulders slumped. "I guess I was. My daddy didn't really accept me so why should they?" Tears coursed down her cheeks.

A fierce sense of protectiveness over-whelmed Kim. She embraced her daughter in a tight hug. "That's their loss. You're special, and they can't change that." She held Anna as she sobbed against Kim's chest.

Kim felt her life was crumbling as she listened to her daughter's sorrow. How could she forgive a man for doing this to his daughter?

Slowly Anna's crying subsided, but she still clung to Kim. Staring into the dark-ness, she noticed the rain had lessened. This storm would push through and move on to another place. She wished life's problems would disappear as easily.

"I love you, Mom. I'm not gonna let Lily's words bother me anymore." She pulled back.

Kim fingered Anna's hair out of her face. "When you start to feel down about what Lily said, just remember how impor-tant you are to us."

"I'm starved. What's Maggie fixing for dinner?"

"I don't know. Let's go in and find out." Kim hooked her arm around Anna, and they headed for the door into the game room.

"I got the last laugh today with Lily. I beat her at one-on-one. She's always bragging about how good she is."

"Where did y'all play?"

"Broussard Park. They have the best courts."

"It has the best view, too." Kim opened the door, and they entered the house.

Laughter filled the room. She came to a stop and stared at her dad, Zane and Maggie laughing together at the other end where the couch and lounge chairs were. Before she could remark on the unusual sight, Zane looked up and snagged her gaze. He winked and motioned for Anna and her to join them.

"You should hear the stories your father is telling about you and Maggie as little girls."

"Stories? What kind?"

"That time you went deep-sea fishing and fell into the water trying to reel your fish in," Maggie answered, swiping the tears from her cheeks.

"That's not funny." Kim set her fist on her hip. "I could have drowned."

Her father pooh-poohed her remark. "You can swim like a fish. What was so funny was you wouldn't let go of your fishing rod. Even in the water you were determined to bring your catch in."

"Sure. I'd saved my money for a whole month to buy that rod—state-of-the-art fishing gear. Just to set the record straight, I did bring in my fish. It was a small shark."

Anna's eyes rounded. "A shark? You were in the water with a shark?"

"It was maybe two feet long. But sharks love to put up a fight. Even small ones."

"Papa Keith, where were you?"

Her father tried to stop chuckling, but it took a moment to compose himself even to answer Anna. "I ran to get the life pre-server to throw to Kim."

"Why didn't you jump in to save her?"

Maggie's laughter increased. "Because at that time Uncle Keith couldn't swim."

Anna's eyes grew even bigger. "You couldn't swim?"

"I can now. You've seen me. But back then, no. I used to be scared of the water."

"What changed your mind?"

"Seeing Kim in the water and knowing if I went in after her I would make things worse. Right after that, I took swimming lessons and slowly overcame my fear of swimming."

Anna plopped down next to Zane on the couch. "I can't imagine not swimming. I love to."

"Well, so did your mom—which that day was a good thing since I wasn't very useful in rescuing her."

"You got the life preserver." Maggie rose and started across the room toward the kitchen area. "Which is how she man-aged to bring the shark in. She held on to that thing and reeled the line in until you could gaff it."

"Yup and we had shark steak that evening. Some of the best I've had." Her dad relaxed back against his chair and finished the last swallow of coffee.

A clap of thunder boomed at the same time lightning struck. Kim yanked around toward the loud sound. "That was close. Too close." She breathed in several deep inhalations, trying to calm the rapid speed of her heartbeat. "I thought it was moving away from us."

Then suddenly another lightning/thunder combination shook the house as though it had blasted through the walls.

Zane surged to his feet. "That's even closer."

He marched toward the door into the hallway. Kim followed right behind him. Going from room to room, he flipped on the light and checked each one.

Kim hurried to keep up with him. "Maybe it struck a tree."

"It struck something nearby. I'm going downstairs to see."

"I'm coming with you. I can cover half the house while you do the other half."

She made her way through the lower floor, finding nothing suspicious. As she approached the staircase again, her breathing evened out. Zane pushed back the plastic sheets and emerged from the living room, his calm expression reassuring her.

"I can go outside and look around, see if I can find any damage."

"I'll go, too." Ascending the steps in front of him, Kim drew in the aromas saturating the air. "The beef stew and—" She took another deep breath. "I smell something else." Halting, she spun toward Zane. "Smoke!"

Chapter Twelve

Zane charged up the remaining stairs, inhaling. "Where's it coming from?"

"Don't know. To be safe, I'm getting everyone out of the house." Kim rushed down the hall.

"I'm taking a look to see if I can find the source of this smoke. Call 911."

"Y'all need to get out of here. We smell smoke," she said as soon as she burst into the game room.

Maggie whirled around at the stove. "The lightning struck the house?"

"It must have. We couldn't find where, though. Zane's still looking."

Anna helped her grandfather to stand, all color drained from both of their faces. "Can we get anything?"

"If it's in here, yes. Otherwise, no. I want you outside." Kim dug into her pocket for her cell.

Maggie grabbed her purse and Kim's, then corralled Keith and Anna toward the exit. "You can't stay," she called back over her shoulder.

"I'm coming." The 911 operator came on the line, and Kim gave her the information, then swung toward the door into the hallway. There was no way she was leaving until Zane was. She hurried down the corridor, yelling his name.

"I'm in here." He came out of her bedroom, sniffing the air. "It's getting stronger. I've searched up here and can't find the source."

Kim stopped in the middle of the upstairs. "The fire department is coming." Drawing in deep breaths, she turned in a full circle.

Her gaze latched on to the door to the

attic. She raced for it, paused and put her hand on it to feel for heat. When it didn't feel hot, she started to open the door. She had it cracked when Zane ran up behind her and slammed it closed. In that second, smoke slithered from the small opening and continued to ooze from the bottom.

He grabbed her hand and tugged her away. "Let's get out of here."

As they hastened toward the exit, her heart pounded until she thought it would come out of her chest. Its frantic beating thundered in her head. *Not again. We can't lose our family home. We were just getting it fixed.*

Huddled in a blanket from a neighbor, Kim leaned against Zane's black truck while her father and Anna sat inside it. A few feet away Maggie talked with Polly's dad while Zane conversed with Gideon, dressed in his fire gear.

The chill of the evening reflected the cold embedded deep into Kim's bones. The scent of smoke and burning wood saturated the air. In the lights shining to illuminate the scene, she glimpsed plumes of smoke drifting toward the black sky, but at least the flames were out. The fire-fighters continued to douse the upper level of Bienville, squashing the last burning embers.

Hopelessness settled over her shoulders as though the rain still fell and drenched the blanket about her. All the past weeks' hard work on renovating the second floor was for nothing. Most of the first floor remained intact, but water soaked and smoke permeated. After the hurricane, they were able to stay in a small part of the house. Now they wouldn't have any place to live—at least for a while.

The trembling in her legs sent her sinking toward the ground. Zane clasped her and held her up. "I know this looks bad—"

"Bad?" She clutched the folds of the blanket and rounded on him. "That's not a strong enough word. My home is gone. We have no place to go. What am I going to do about Dad?"

He grasped both of her arms and tugged her farther away from the truck. "I've called Cody to be here in case your dad needs him. I will help you. You are not alone in this. Do you hear me?"

Yes, she heard his words, but they failed to sink in. She could only stare at her childhood home, a house that had withstood one hundred fifty years of time. She couldn't understand why this was happening to her. What had she done to deserve this?

Why, God?

"Kim? Your family needs you to be strong."

Zane's words reached her. "Strong? I'm not allowed to fall apart?"

He slung his arm around her shoulder and walked her toward one of Maggie's newly planted gardens, away from the lights and the people gathered.

"Yes, you can. I'm here to listen."

"Why now? Why me?" Welling tears made any more words impossible to say.

"Sometimes there isn't an answer for

those questions. I know during the hurricane many people were asking themselves those questions. All I can say is life is never a smooth road. There are bumps and detours and even holes we encounter along the way."

She swallowed the lump. "I feel like I've fallen into a crater. I'm at the bottom looking up into pitch blackness. I'm even afraid to grasp on and start my climb out for fear I'll be—" her throat constricted, and she gulped back the emotions rising to take over "—knocked down again."

He pressed her against him and wrapped his arms about her. "I'm here for you this time. If I have to, I'll climb down into the crater and help you up every step of the way."

His soothing words unleashed her sorrow, and the tears flowed unchecked down her cheeks. As the water from the hoses splashed down onto her home, her sobs splashed down onto his shirt as he held her to him.

* * *

"I don't want us to be a burden." Kim poured Ruth a cup of coffee from the pot Kim had made earlier. She hadn't been able to sleep at all and had finally gotten up and come downstairs to the kitchen.

"My dear, I love having you stay here with me. I have the room now that Kathleen and my grandsons are living with Gideon. So don't think you're imposing one bit." Ruth peered toward Kim's dad. "This'll give your dad and me a chance to work on the campaign. The election is in a few days."

"We're grateful for your hospitality." Kim's father sat at the end of the kitchen table in Ruth's house, black circles under his eyes, lines of weariness on his face, but his gaze was clear, not blank and distant like after the hurricane.

Kim appreciated the fact that Ruth was helping take her dad's mind off the fire that had consumed the attic and part of the second story of Bienville. "Zane said something about getting us a trailer to use in a few days."

"Nonsense. I hate you staying in a trailer when I have the space." Ruth leaned toward Kim and lowered her voice. "Don't tell my daughter that I miss her and the boys, but I do. I got used to the noise level being loud. This past week has been too quiet."

"After the fire department says it's okay, I'll need to assess the damage. Zane will help me with that. It's just that…" She couldn't say anything else. All the words had been said—and the tears shed—the night before to Zane who had finally brought her dad, Anna and her to Ruth's to stay while Maggie and Brady went to stay with a cousin.

"The minute Gideon called to let me know what was happening, I started preparing the bedrooms upstairs. I wasn't going to take no for an answer." Ruth patted Kim's father's hand. "I couldn't have done this campaign without you,

Keith. This is the least I can do for you and your family."

He gave Ruth a weary smile that brightened his eyes for a few seconds. As he lifted his cup to his mouth, his hands trembled, but the brief grin lifted Kim's spirits. Cody had arrived at the fire and had talked with her father for forty-five minutes while Kim had consoled Anna. Zane had been right. She couldn't allow herself to fall apart. That short time with Zane last night was all the time she would let herself mourn the loss of her house. She had to hold the family together. If they had to tear down Bienville, then she would deal with it. If they could repair it, then she would manage that, too. At least that was what she'd told herself in the early morning hours when she couldn't sleep. But now the prospects of the road ahead—after the past months of dealing with the damage from the hurricane and her father's failing health—made her want to retreat from life, get in the car and drive until she ran out of gas and money. She wasn't a chuck-it-all kind of person, but the temptation was great.

When Kim centered her attention on Ruth and her dad at the end of the table talking between themselves, the strong connection developing between them shouldn't have taken her by surprise but it did. Her father looked tired, understandably, but not defeated. Something else stunned her, though. He lifted his hand and grazed it along Ruth's jawline, his eyes sparkling. What was transpiring between them was more than friendship. She'd known that but not the depth of it. When did this happen?

Kim scooted back her chair and stood. "I think I'm going out to the house."

Her dad glanced toward her and said, "Do you want me to come?" Then he returned his gaze to Ruth.

"No. I thought I would check what's happening. Get some kind of estimate from the fire department. I couldn't see everything last night when we left." She strode toward the hallway that led to the staircase. She couldn't stay any longer in the kitchen because she felt like an outsider. Ruth and her dad needed privacy.

Upstairs she eased the door open into the guest bedroom and found her daughter still sleeping. Tiptoeing to the dresser, Kim grabbed her purse, the only item other than the clothes on her back that she had with her from the house.

Leaving Anna asleep, she went down the stairs, rummaging in her purse for her keys until she realized her car was in the detached garage at Bienville. She considered asking Ruth to use her car but decided not to. It was only two miles to her house and she could use the walk.

She peered up. The bright blue sky without one cloud mocked her mood. As she began her trek toward her house, nature continued to taunt her with its joyous beauty and cycle of renewal as a pair of cardinals flew back and forth with twigs to build their nest, flowers bloomed and the trees filled in with leaves.

She strolled on the sidewalk that ran

beside the highway between the houses and the sea. The mirror-smooth water glittered in the sun beginning its ascent. The scent of the Gulf's salty tang and flowers in full glory along her way urged her to let go of her sorrow, and she nearly did until she turned into the long driveway that led to Bienville. That was when she saw the house, and new tears crowded her eyes until she could hardly see.

She stopped, frozen.

The enormity of what she had ahead of her struck her in full force. Some of the second floor was gone, as well as the whole attic. All the boxes of memories stored on the third level vanished in the fire. The antebellum gown that she'd worn to the Mardi Gras party had been her mother's and stored in the attic—not to mention some of the antique furniture they had moved since the roof had been repaired so they could renovate the downstairs.

Behind her she heard a vehicle pull up and stop. She didn't have the energy even to turn and see who had arrived. Her gaze stayed fastened on the charred remains of the upper part of her home. The slam of a door jolted her out of her daze. Slowly she turned toward the newcomer. Seeing Zane's dad, she sniffed back the tears and straightened her shoulders.

Then she spied the sheen in his eyes and the dam holding back her tears broke. Wet tracks rolled down her cheeks.

A couple of feet from her, he said, "I'm so sorry that this happened to Bienville, Kim. It has such beauty and history. I had to come first thing this morning. I was praying what I saw last night had been a nightmare."

"So had I."

He took a step. She took a step. And then she was in his arms, seeking comfort from a man who at one time she couldn't forgive. Now he was giving her solace when he certainly had good reasons to be leery of her and her family.

Vaguely she heard another vehicle stop and a door shut. She quickly composed herself. When she looked up, she glimpsed Zane. The expression of sympathy nearly undid her all over again. He reached out to her, and she went into his embrace.

"I went by Ruth's to get you, but she said you'd already left for here."

"I couldn't sit around there any longer. I needed to know how bad it is."

Zane glanced beyond her. "I'm not gonna kid you. It looks bad, but Gideon thinks the floor to the second floor is sound. The fire didn't reach there. It did damage part of the walls, though—" he waved toward the house "—as you can see."

"When can we go upstairs and see for ourselves?"

"Gideon thinks by midafternoon."

"I'm going up to the house to look around," Tom said then left her and Zane alone.

After his dad drove away, he rubbed his hands up and down her arms. "I can't imagine what you are going through, but—"

Before he could say any more, she said, "No, you can't." She backed away. She was tired of depending on others for help. She could never repay Zane for all he'd done for her and her family. And now it would start all over again.

"I know you're hurting. I know you feel defeated. You don't think I've experienced those feelings?"

"I'm sure you have—under different circumstances. Up until last night I'd begun to feel that I was getting my life back together, that my dad would heal and regain a semblance of what he was at one time. Last night that went up in flames—literally. The battle starts all over again, and I'm plain tired of fighting." She swung around and marched toward Bienville.

Zane dogged her steps. "Why don't you wait and come back later? Let's go to breakfast and then church. Give yourself some space."

She wheeled around, and he nearly collided into her. "No, I want to be alone. I'm going to get my car and go somewhere to think. Is that enough space for you?"

He yanked back as if she'd slapped him in the face. "Fine. I'll see you here at three this afternoon." Pivoting, he stalked to his truck and backed out of the driveway onto the highway.

Kim curled her hands until her fingernails dug into her palms. Numb, she hardly felt the pain. After he disappeared from her view, she continued her way to the detached garage. She refused to look in the direction of her burnt home. But she didn't need to. The image was seared into her thoughts.

Standing in her bedroom at her house, Kim listened to Zane tell her what he could do to repair the damage. She peered up at the blue sky exposed through the holes and missing sections of the roof— again. Zane's voice faded from her consciousness. The view threw her back almost five months ago when the hurricane hit and she walked into her room the first time to see the destruction.

When she finally looked at Zane, he'd quit talking, his gaze on her. "Whatever you think is fine with me. You're the expert." Her shoulders hunched as she crossed her arms over her chest.

"Has your insurance agent said when the adjuster will come out?"

"He thought tomorrow sometime."

Zane picked his way through the wet debris to her. "I'll take care of it if that's okay. I know how overwhelmed you feel right now."

She opened her mouth.

He held up his hand and quickly said, "I've dealt with many others in similar situations, Kim. The good news is your downstairs isn't in too bad shape. We'll deal with the water and smoke, but structurally it is sound. I know you want to retain as much of the old house as possible."

"If it wasn't for Dad, I'd walk away. I don't have what it takes to fight anymore."

Beyond the destruction to the house, most of their personal belongings had been burnt or damaged beyond use.

She pivoted and started for the hallway. She needed to get out of the house. Her gaze latched on to a photo of her and Anna lying on the floor near the dresser where it had sat. The glass was shattered and the picture ruined. Hurrying, she escaped into the corridor and continued to the staircase.

The stench of smoke and burnt wood drove her outside. Her stomach roiled as she increased her pace. She gulped down the bile rising in her throat and strode toward her car. She'd been away from her dad and Anna long enough.

"Kim." At her car, Zane touched her shoulder. "I've been calling your name."

She slanted a look toward him as his hand slipped from her, and he came around between her and her car. "I didn't hear you."

"And that's what has me worried. Please talk to me."

She fumbled for her keys in her pocket. "I don't have any words to say to anyone. I need to get home to Dad and Anna. I'll talk to you later."

His penetratingly intense gaze bored into her, then he stepped to the side, opening her car door for her. "I'll come by later tonight. There are details we need to work out about the house at least."

"Sure," she mumbled and slipped behind the steering wheel.

As she drove away, she saw Zane watching her leave, a frown on his face, his brow creased with concern. He cared and at the moment she didn't. Not about anything.

The pain Zane glimpsed in Kim's eyes pierced through him, but there wasn't anything more he could do. He would repair her home, and he would be here for her. But she was pushing away, shutting down.

No, he'd never had his house burn, but he knew what it was like to hit rock bottom and just want to hide in the darkness, to hope that nothing else happened to shove him down even more. The only way he'd crawled out of that hole had been through the Lord. He'd finally realized years ago he couldn't do it alone. He had to lean on God.

Please, Father, help Kim to see You are the answer to her problems. You are her strength in times like this.

Evening descended all around Kim as she sat on Ruth's back deck, the darkness giving a chill to the air. She pulled her sweater around her, relishing the quiet and peace after dealing with a parade of people offering their prayers and condolences. Most had been optimistic, especially with Zane's company rebuilding the upper level. Even their insurance agent had talked with her father and reassured him that he would prod the company to move fast on this claim. People had brought clothing for them to use and money to help them through the situation—money many couldn't spare because of their own trials since the hurricane.

Kim pushed to her feet and walked to the edge of the deck, leaning into the railing, her hands clutching the wood. She didn't want to be responsible for others going without because of her and her family. Hope had gone through so much in the past months.

I'm asking again, Lord. Why? What am I doing wrong?

The sound of the back door opening and closing drew her around to face Zane, the light from the window revealing his solemn expression.

"Your dad said you were out here. He seems to be all right. I'm glad."

"That won't last. He's putting on a show for Ruth." Each time she had talked with her father, Ruth had been near, but she intended to talk with him in private later tonight. She needed to be sure he wouldn't fall apart again. "He was that way after the hurricane, too, putting up a front for everyone."

"Did Cody come by today? He said he was going to."

"Yes, while I was gone. He stayed about an hour."

Zane moved toward her. "It might not hurt for you to talk to Cody."

"I'll be okay. It's my family I'm worried about."

"So the house burning doesn't bother you?" He positioned himself next to her and stared out into the backyard, away from the light shining onto the deck.

She couldn't see his facial features well and wondered if he'd done that on purpose. "What do you think? Of course, it bothers me, but I can't allow myself to give in to those feelings. Someone has to hold the family together."

"But what about you?" He tilted his head toward her, throwing his profile into the light. "You aren't allowed to feel sad, angry, hurt?"

"What do you want me to say?"

"The truth. That this is killing you. You

are at a loss. You're struggling and need help."

"No one can help me. What I'm feeling is what I'm feeling. You can't change that."

"You're right. And I wouldn't. You need to have those feelings, work through them and move on. That won't happen unless you acknowledge them. Give them over to the Lord. Fighting the circumstances and Him can be too much for one person." He turned toward her, cutting the gap between them in half. "I love you, and I'll be here for you when you need me."

The words of the last sentence washed through her, leaving in their wake fear of adding more hurt to what she was experiencing. He'd left her once. What was to stop him from doing that again when something didn't go the way he wanted? She was afraid any more rejections would pull her apart at the seams. For Anna and her dad, she couldn't afford to make any mistakes.

She backed away. "No, don't do that."

Chapter Thirteen

"Don't do what?" Zane asked, watching Kim pull herself up as tall as she could.

"Don't love me. We had our chance. The time for us is over." She spun on her heel and hurried toward the back door.

"Kim."

She kept going into the house. The banging of the screen door sent a jolt through Zane.

What in the world had possessed him to declare his love at such a bad time? He'd wanted to wipe her pain away. He'd wanted her to know she wasn't alone, that he would be here for her. He'd wanted her to know he'd fallen in love with her even against his better judgment.

But to Kim it was too late for them. Maybe she was right. Their time had been years ago, and he'd blown it back then. Now he had to live with the consequences.

"Zane, what's wrong with Kim? She flew through the living room and out the front door, saying she was going for a walk." Keith walked out onto the deck. "Normally that wouldn't concern me except for how she's been behaving today and the look on her face."

"What kind of look?"

"Oddly if I had to say, a mixture of anger and sadness. I'm just glad Anna decided to go to her room and didn't see her mother like this. Is there some bad news you aren't telling me about the house? You said it could be repaired."

"It can. And no, I haven't withheld anything from you."

"Then what happened?" Keith leaned back against the railing.

"I told your daughter I love her."

"And that caused her to run out the front door?"

"I guess so. She thinks our time is over, and maybe she's right. I don't know anymore where she is concerned, but don't worry. I am still going to do the best job with your house. My father has taken a personal interest in making sure it is restored. Now if you'll excuse me, I'd better get home. I'll have to make arrangements tomorrow for a full crew to work on Bienville."

Zane made it to the back door when Keith's words stopped him. "Thank you for all you've done. I was so wrong all those years ago, and my daughter hopefully will discover that."

But that might be too late. Zane kept the words to himself as he strode through the house and left.

Later that night, Kim let herself into Ruth's house and started toward the staircase.

"Kim, is that you?" her dad asked from the living room.

"Yes." She went to him. "Is everyone else in bed?" She checked her watch and noted it was ten.

"Yes, but I couldn't sleep. Wanted to make sure you were all right."

"I'm fine. You shouldn't stay up because of me. I went for a walk and ended up in town at the café."

"You're walking a lot lately."

"It's good exercise." And a way for her to work off her anger.

"Do you have a few minutes to talk?"

"I guess. What do you need?"

"For you to sit down." Her father waved his hand toward the chair across from him.

She took it, perching herself on its edge. "Did something happen while I was gone?"

"No. With the election soon, Ruth and I were going over our last-minute strategy. I don't think she has anything to be concerned about, but she worries, anyway.

Worry can be tough on a person, don't you think?"

"Well, yes." She studied her dad's unreadable expression. What was he up to?

"Cody is teaching me that. I think you should talk to him. He's a good counselor."

"Why aren't you upset about what happened last night? You sound so calm."

"Again Cody. He's helping me to put the situation in perspective."

"But our home? It will be months before we can return to it."

"Zane assures me he'll work as fast as he can to get it repaired. He thinks he can have part of it ready for us in six to eight weeks. In the meantime, Ruth wants us to stay here."

"You're okay with that?"

"I'd rather do that than stay in a trailer. Wouldn't you?"

"I'd rather have our house back," she blurted out before censoring herself. She didn't want to stir up her dad.

"That's not an option."

"And that doesn't bother you?"

"What do you want me to say? Yes, it bothers me. Can I do anything about what happened? No. I couldn't accept what occurred with the hurricane, which made my health decline. I'm not going to do that again. I can't control everything. I admit that. That doesn't mean I like it. It just means I'm going to stop fighting that fact. Let it go, Kim."

She came to her feet. "I'm trying. It's not that easy."

"I agree, but you're the only one who can decide that for yourself."

"I'm going to bed. There's a lot to do tomorrow."

She sought the refuge of her bedroom she was sharing with Anna. While she got ready for bed in the semidarkness of the nightlight, she couldn't understand why she seemed to be the only one in her family upset about the fire. So much of their belongings would have to be thrown out. Weary, she sank onto the mattress next to her sleeping daughter. She was tired of starting her life over—when Zane left her the first time, when she married Scott and then again when he walked out, and when the hurricane hit. And now the fire threatened the one stable aspect of her life the family had managed to retain over the years. Bienville. How could she pick up the pieces and start anew?

Tuesday evening, Kim reluctantly attended the watch party for Ruth's mayoral bid at the Bay Shore Hotel. She certainly didn't feel like celebrating after the insurance adjuster had given her the news she had expected. The age of their house made it impossible to get replacement costs for damaged areas. She would continue to negotiate with the company, but whatever amount they settled upon wouldn't cover everything they needed. If she accepted Zane's help, which he insisted on giving, she would be tied to him—indebted to him.

In the ballroom, the festive atmosphere urged her to forget her problems for the night, but then she spied Zane across the room, looking handsome in tan slacks, a light blue shirt and a darker blue tie. He was leaving tomorrow for Nashville and to discuss his project with the Christian Assistance Coalition. In her gut, she knew he would get their approval and be called away from Hope. That was why she needed to keep her distance. She could never leave Hope.

Maggie stepped next to Kim. "Ruth is about to make her victory speech. It's about time. It was obvious hours ago she would win."

"She's being cautious—probably my dad's influence. He once knew a candidate who declared himself the winner too early and lost the race."

"Ruth needed his expertise. This past month there's been a buzz about town concerning her."

Kim's eyes searched the crowd and lit upon her father standing with Ruth. "Yeah, Dad did a great job. I don't think he ever thought about running a campaign." Since he'd begun working with Ruth and talking with Cody, her father had changed. He still had tremors and got frustrated, but he was so much calmer. Instead of hiding at home, he put himself out there with others.

"Which is a good thing. This will make it easier for you."

Kim peered at her cousin. "Easier?"

"To move on with your life."

"Move on? I'm doing what I want. I love teaching. And we'll get Bienville repaired and move back into the house. "

"What about Zane?"

Kim scanned the area and noticed a few people nearby who could overhear their conversation. "There's nothing to say." She turned toward the front of the ballroom where Ruth mounted the stage and stood behind the podium. "Ruth's about to speak."

"You aren't going to get off that easy. We'll resume this later," Maggie whispered next to Kim's ear.

Ten minutes later, Ruth stepped down

from the stage into the midst of well-wishers congratulating her on winning. Kim's father stood next to Ruth—like they were a couple. Was he moving on? For years after her mother had died, he'd been lost without his wife. Was Ruth and Dad's friendship blossoming into something more permanent?

Kim glanced to her side and noticed Maggie had gone. When Kim turned back, her gaze collided with Zane's. He threaded his way through the people in the ballroom until he stopped in front of her.

Without preamble, he discussed his plan for the house repair. "Now that we've got the go-ahead from the insurance adjuster, I'm starting tomorrow first thing. We'll get the house reroofed first before working on the interior."

She lifted one corner of her mouth. "It seems like you just did that."

The hard edge to his eyes softened. "Yeah. Before long I could do it in my sleep." He averted his gaze for a few sec-

onds then met hers. "I'm leaving tomorrow afternoon for Nashville. Dad will be
in charge of the crew, so if you have any
questions, talk with him."

Good. Since Tom had been repairing
Bienville, they had come to an under-
standing. She respected him for pulling
his life together and for his skills working
on the house. He had an eye for bringing
out the historical appeal of a place. Their
once adversarial relationship had evolved
until now she could call him a friend. At
one time, that would have surprised her.
"I will."

"Kim, we should…" But he didn't finish
what he was going to say. Instead, he
nodded once then moved away from her.

She almost went after him, but what
would she say to him? I care for you? I
love you? No, she couldn't. Years ago
when he left her, she'd thrown herself
into a relationship with Scott and that
had ended badly for not just herself but
several others in her life. Her judgment
had been skewed because she had looked

to another for a solution to her problem. She wasn't going to do that now. What if she was wrong about Zane? She couldn't make that kind of mistake again. She had others to consider besides herself.

"Anna has already been complaining that this is her last year to enjoy searching for candy at the church Easter egg hunt," Kim said to Kathleen in Broussard Park across the street from Hope Community Church on Sunday after the service.

"Kip said almost those exact words. Do you think they've been talking about it?"

Kim glanced at the pair hunting for the eggs near the basketball court where the older kids were searching. "Yes, and it doesn't surprise me. They've been spending a lot of time together since we've been staying at your mom's."

"You know our parents have a thing for each other."

Kim chuckled, surveying the crowd across the park. Ruth and her dad stood side by side holding hands. "Hard not to see it. I feel like their chaperone."

"And I'm glad or we could have a scandal before Mom even takes office in April." Kathleen laughed.

"I'm thrilled she won the election. She's done so much for us, especially my father."

Shielding her eyes, Kathleen angled toward Kim. "I could say the same thing about your father. Until he became her campaign manager, she was doing things halfheartedly. He inspired her, gave her what she needed to become enthused about running for mayor. He's got a gift and insight into campaigning."

"Yeah, I feel like I'm getting my dad back. I'm glad he's happy with your mother."

"So what about you?" By stepping in front of Kim, Kathleen blocked her view of the festivities of a hundred children running around trying to find treats before the others. "I've seen you and Zane together. You can't tell me you don't have feelings for him—like when you and I were in high school."

"It's more complicated now. I have to think of my daughter and Dad."

"Zane is wonderful with my children."

"He once told me he didn't want to have children. I know that his relationship with his father is much better now, but I don't…" She couldn't finish the sentence because she didn't really know how Zane felt since he and his father had become closer.

"Being a parent, as you well know, is scary. No matter what he says, he'd do a great job—" Kathleen pointed toward the park "—and Anna adores him."

Kim peered at her daughter talking with Zane. Her Easter basket was full, overflowing with chocolate and candy. Anna kept bending down and picking up pieces that fell out of her basket. Zane directed her toward the sidelines while the other children continued hunting. But Anna didn't seem to mind. She laughed at something Zane said, set her stash on the ground then sat beside it to begin eating her treats.

Kim had made it a point to avoid him as much as she could. When she did see him at her house checking the progress of the work, she would start to dream about what could have been between them. With a shake of her head, she looked away from Zane.

"His dad told me he's partnering with the Christian Assistance Coalition to start his foundation for housing needed in areas of destruction. His life is going to be very busy. I won't be surprised if he moves away. Zane is a hands-on kind of guy. I don't see him turning it over to just anyone to oversee," Kim said, more to convince herself than Kathleen.

"What's holding you here?"

"I love Hope. I've lived here all my life. Dad needs me." She threw out one reason after another, but the words didn't really ring true to her. "Anna loves it here, too," Kim said, throwing out one last argument but keeping the real one deep inside.

Kathleen studied her for a long moment. "I see you're trying to fit everything into a nice little box. Life is so much simpler when it doesn't suddenly change."

"Like with the hurricane?"

She nodded. "One day we had a beautiful small town on the Gulf. The next day our house washed away or took in water. I lost almost all of our possessions when my house was swept away."

"How did you handle it?"

"By leaning on Gideon. He taught me to renew my faith in the Lord. God is my strength. If I can't control my life—and I can't—I'm glad it is in His hands. Let your insecurities and fears go. Life is too short to worry all the time."

In the middle of the field, children sat on the grass, digging into their baskets and unwrapping their candy. Zane planted himself in their midst supervising them, making sure no child went without his share. He was good with kids, she reminded herself again. He should be a father.

"You see it, don't you?" Kathleen asked.

Kim didn't have to ask what Kathleen meant. "Yeah."

"Go talk to him."

"I can't. I—"

"Do you love him?"

"Yes, but it's not that simple. I loved him fifteen years ago, and he left me."

"You've never forgiven him, have you?"

She started to say, "Yes, of course I have," but she realized if she examined her heart she couldn't really answer that truthfully. Instead, she said, "No, not like I should have."

"First you need to do that. Everything else will fall into place after that."

Later that afternoon, she heard Zane calling her name as she stood in the middle of her bedroom upstairs at Bienville. She went into the hallway and leaned over the banister. "I'm up here."

He appeared at the bottom of the staircase. Wariness guarded his expression while he made his way to the second floor.

"Dad told me everything was going well. Is there a problem?"

"Yes, there is."

His forehead crinkled. "What?"

"I've been doing things all wrong."

"With the house?"

"No, with you." She grabbed his hand and tugged him toward her bedroom. "You see this room?"

"Yeah." He sent her a puzzled look.

"When I used to look at it, I thought it was my home. Where I grew up. Where I would always live. I used to think this house grounded me. Kept me focused on what was important—family and tradition. I was wrong. Now all I see is just a room. One day it will be a nice bedroom again but just a bedroom. No more, no less."

"Why are you telling me this?"

"After talking with Kathleen earlier at the egg hunt, I started thinking about what she asked me. She wanted to know if I forgave you for leaving all those years ago."

Both of his eyebrows rose.

"In the end, I had to tell her no. I'd been holding on to a small part of my anger and fear. I couldn't quite let go and forgive you totally because that would mean I would be free to feel again. And I was scared of my feelings. Didn't trust them."

Skepticism darkened his eyes. "You do now?"

She inhaled then exhaled a deep breath. "I'm trusting God. For so long I've tried hard to control my life because I didn't want to go through the kind of marriage and divorce I had with Scott again. The Lord has shown me I'm not in control really. Life changes sometimes quickly and unexpectedly. But through all of that I won't be alone. I like that feeling. It's kind of freeing not to feel I have to control everything for it to work."

"I'm glad for you. You'll be happier."

He said all the right words, but he remained a few feet away from her, his arms crossed over his chest. Had she lost his love? Was it too late? She fortified herself with another deep breath and said, "I love you, Zane. I know now I never stopped. I hope I can play a part in your life."

He held his ground, and she worried it was too late for them. "You know the foundation was approved, right?"

She nodded. "I'm glad. It's needed."

"What if I wanted to travel for the first year or so getting it started and training the right team?"

"You should. I'll be behind you all the way."

Finally he stepped closer and said the words she wanted to hear. "I love you. I want us to marry. Are you willing to leave Hope for me?"

"Yes," she said without hesitation. "Because I love you and where you are is my home. Not this place."

"What about Anna?"

"She can go, too. I can homeschool her. She'll learn so much traveling, being involved with your project. It'll be an adventure."

His gaze penetrated through any barriers she'd erected as though he could peek into her heart and see her true intent. Suddenly a smile graced his mouth, and he closed the space between them. "You really mean it?"

"You know me. I wouldn't say it unless I did. I'm tired of being alone. I want a partner, someone who will love me through the bad times, as well as the good."

He slid his arms around her and tugged her nearer. "Ma'am, I'm up for that job."

She rose up on her tiptoes and brushed her lips across his. "You're okay with being a father? Because Anna needs one."

"Okay? I'm ecstatic."

She leaned back. "You'd consider more children?"

"Once we aren't traveling so much. Give me a year to get the project up and running, and then you can have your way with me."

She laughed, and Zane kissed the laughter from her lips.

Epilogue

Two months later

For years Bienville hadn't been decked out in such colorful grandeur as it was today, the day of Kim's wedding to Zane. She came down the staircase after changing into her traveling clothes to find everyone, including her husband, standing on the ground floor of the family's renovated antebellum home. Cheers rose as she descended toward Zane.

She fit her hand in his, and they faced their family and friends who had been invited to the reception at Bienville. She skimmed over the smiling faces of her dad, Ruth, Maggie, Brady, and Zane's father and finally rested her gaze on Anna. Her daughter beamed, dressed in a beautiful yellow dress. Kim signaled to Anna who rushed toward her and threw her arms around her and Zane.

"Bring me something back from St. John, please."

"We will. You aren't gonna give Papa Keith any grief, are you?" Zane asked what Kim identified as a serious fatherly voice.

Anna giggled. "Ruth won't let me get away with anything."

"I know. But I had to ask." Zane winked at his new daughter.

She turned to Kim. "I'll do my homework while you're gone, and Papa Keith is going to work with me on my math and reading."

"Good because when we get back from our honeymoon, we'll need to be ready to leave at a moment's notice. It's hurricane season." Kim leaned down, hugged Anna then kissed her cheek.

Anna smiled. "Susan caught your bouquet. Do you think she'll get married next? I was hoping Maggie would."

"You never know, especially since Dad and Ruth eloped last month."

Tossing his head toward the crowd that parted to let them leave, Zane captured Kim's hand. "Ready to run the gauntlet?"

"I've been ready for fifteen years." With her husband by her side, Kim hurried toward the waiting limousine in front of Bienville and toward her future with the man she loved.

* * * * *

Dear Reader,

This is the second story in the A Town Called Hope series. Hope has experienced a hurricane that destroyed a good part of the town. I grew up in an area where hurricanes strike—along the Gulf Coast in Mississippi. I have seen firsthand the damage a hurricane can do and the way a town can pull together to rebuild. I have written this series as a tribute to the people who have dealt with a tragedy and have come out stronger. Even if we can't personally go to a place that has been hit with a hurricane, tornado or earthquake, we can give money through a charitable organization and we can pray for the people.

I love hearing from readers. You can contact me at margaretdaley@gmail.com, or at P.O. Box 2074, Tulsa, OK 74101. You can also learn more about my books at www.margaretdaley.com. I have a quarterly newsletter that you can sign up for on my website, or you can enter my monthly drawings by signing my guestbook.

Best wishes,

Margaret Daley

Questions for Discussion

1. Kim has had two people abandon her—her first love, Zane, and her husband. She is scared to trust when she meets Zane again. Her past rules her life. Do you have something that has happened in your past that has done that to you? How can you get past that?

2. Who is your favorite character? Why?

3. In this story, the importance of forgiving is explored. Why is it important to forgive others and ourselves? What happens when we live in the past rather than looking to the future? Which do you focus on—past, present or future? Why?

4. Kim felt that if her ancestral home was repaired, her life would get back on track. She'd made that paramount in her life. She lost focus on the im-

portance of God in her life. Have you done this? How did you resolve the problem?

5. What is your favorite scene? Why?

6. Kim rushed into a marriage because her family approved of the man, and she realized she'd made a big mistake within six months of marrying him. She stuck with her marriage, but eventually her husband left her and her one-month-old baby, damaging her family's business, as well. Her bad choice led to many repercussions that hurt her and her family. Have you ever made the kind of mistake you felt that you paid for more than most? How did you deal with it?

7. Kim thought if she could control her life, then she would be all right. She didn't realize there are a lot of things we can't control in our lives. What are some things that have happened to you

lately that have been out of your control? How did you deal with them?

8. Zane didn't have a good relationship with his father. His dad was an alcoholic who wasn't a good father. Zane didn't want to be a father because of the example he had growing up. How do parents influence their children while they are growing up? If you are in a bad situation, does that mean you will repeat those mistakes, or can you break the cycle? Explain your answer.

9. Just as Kim felt they were starting to get back on their feet, a fire destroys the work they had done on their house. Have you ever had continual setbacks like that? If so, how did you deal with them? What got you through?

10. Kim couldn't forgive her husband or Zane for leaving. She knew God wanted her to forgive and move on, but she had a hard time doing that. Have

you ever done something you know you shouldn't? How did the situation turn out?

11. This is a series about hope in time of tragedy. What are some ways we can give hope to another in their time of need?

12. Zane's father struggled with alcoholism. Have you or a loved one dealt with an addiction? How did you cope? What did you do to help yourself or your loved one?

13. Kim's dad had a disease that was causing him a lot of problems. He wasn't doing as well as he used to, and Kim was taking over more of the responsibilities of running the household and finances. How do you treat your parents now that you're an adult? Do health issues affect your interaction with your parents?

14. Both Kim and Zane realized their fathers needed a purpose in life, that their problems had stripped away what purpose they had. Have you ever had that problem with yourself or someone you know? How can you change that? Why is it important that a person feel their life makes a difference?

15. Kim wondered what her life would have been like if Zane hadn't left fifteen years before because he didn't think they came from the same world. Do you ever wonder where you would be today if something had been different in your past? Is it good to wonder "what if" in our lives? Why or why not?